GHOST PIRATES

ALSO EDITED BY TOM MCCARTHY

Incredible Tales of the Sea
Classic Sailing Stories
Incredible Pirate Tales

GHOST PIRATES

and other tales of the high seas

Edited by
Tom McCarthy

THE LYONS PRESS
Guilford, Connecticut

An imprint of The Globe Pequot Press

To buy books in quantity for corporate use
or incentives, call **(800) 962–0973**
or e-mail **premiums@GlobePequot.com**.

The Lyons Press is an imprint of The Globe Pequot Press.

10 9 8 7 6 5 4 3 2 1

Printed in the United States of America

Designed by Sheryl P. Kober

ISBN: 978-1-59921-097-1

Library of Congress Cataloging-in-Publication Data is available on file.

contents

For Valerie, Maggie, and Britta

introduction

Why are ghost stories so enticingly popular? Why do pirate stories, as they have for ages, likewise entertain, excite, and enthrall so many readers? It's fairly simple, I think. These genres provide thrills—and chills—at little cost to and no effort on the part of the reader. All one has to do is find a comfortable chair and hold on for a ripping good scare or a heart-pounding adventure. This collection, I hope, will provide readers, young and old alike, everything they want. The stories contained here are classics, having been read and enjoyed by generations of pirate lovers.

So what do we have in store? In "The Shadow of the Sea," strange things happen as night falls. "I scarcely know how to put it," a mystified and frightened crewman says to his captain. "It's—it's about these—these things."

"What things? Speak out man," he said.

"Well Sir," I blurted out. "There's some dreadful thing or things come aboard this ship, since we left port."

I saw him give one quick glance at the Second mate, and the

Second looked back. Then the Skipper replied.

"How do you mean, come aboard?" he asked.

"Out of the sea, Sir," I said, "I've seen them."

What are these "things" he's referring to? Read on and find out.

You'll also learn how a crew from an English ship encounters the dangers of life on a river in Malaysia in "Among the Malay Pirates." And in the curious case of "The Pirate Who Couldn't Swim," you'll see how a pirate's lack of aquatic skills didn't deter his ability to rob and pillage with the best of them. Then there is the fascinating account of the treacherous and bloodthirsty Edward Teach of Bristol, England, better known as Black Beard, and how he met his bloody end. In the journal found after his death, Black Beard wrote the following: "Such a day, rum all out, our company somewhat sober, a damned confusion among us!—rogues a plotting—great talk of separation. So I looked sharp for a prize,—such a day took one, with a great deal of liquor on board—so kept the company hot, damned hot, then all things went well again."

What is now the peaceful beach town of Lewes, Delaware's oldest town, is also the home for "legends of dark doings of famous pirates, of their mysterious, sinister comings and goings, of treasures buried in the sand dunes and pine barrens back of the cape and along the Atlantic beach to the southward." Read about one such reprobate in "Blueskin the Pirate."

Among other things you'll learn and enjoy are descriptions of the lives of some notorious real-life pirates, such as George Lowther, who set sail from the river Thames in 1721 as a second mate aboard the *Gambia Castle*, bound for Africa. His is a story of great intrigue and adventure—and ultimately for Lowther, an untimely demise. Here also is Thomas Anstis, who plied his violent trade in the West Indies, and John Halsey, a Bostonian with an unquenchable ambition. And did you know that the pirate Captain Kidd actually began his career as a sailor in the British merchant service? Find out how he changed careers in "The Real Captain Kidd."

May the reading of this volume prove as adventurous as the lives of the pirates herein.

Tom McCarthy
Chester, Connecticut
March 2007

chapter 1

The Shadow in the Sea

BY WILLIAM HOPE HODGSON

I went up the ladder, and walked across to where the Skipper and the Second Mate stood talking earnestly, by the rail. Tammy kept behind. As I came near to them, I caught two or three words, though I attached no meaning then to them. They were: ". . . send for him." Then the two of them turned and looked at me, and the Second Mate asked what I wanted.

"I want to speak to you and the Old M—Captain, Sir," I answered.

"What is it, Jessop?" the Skipper inquired.

"I scarcely know how to put it, Sir," I said. "It's—it's about these—these things."

"What things? Speak out, man," he said.

"Well, Sir," I blurted out. "There's some dreadful thing or things come aboard this ship, since we left port."

I saw him give one quick glance at the Second Mate, and the Second looked back.

Then the Skipper replied.

"How do you mean, come aboard?" he asked.

"Out of the sea, Sir," I said. "I've seen them. So's Tammy, here."

"Ah!" he exclaimed, and it seemed to me, from his face, that he was understanding something better. "Out of the sea!"

Again he looked at the Second Mate; but the Second was staring at me.

"Yes Sir," I said. "It's the ship. She's not safe! I've watched. I think I understand a bit; but there's a lot I don't."

I stopped. The Skipper had turned to the Second Mate. The Second nodded, gravely. Then I heard him mutter, in a low voice, and the Old Man replied; after which he turned to me again.

"Look here, Jessop," he said. "I'm going to talk straight to you. You strike me as being a cut above the ordinary shellback, and I think you've sense enough to hold your tongue."

"I've got my mate's ticket, Sir," I said, simply.

Behind me, I heard Tammy give a little start. He had not known about it until then.

The Skipper nodded.

"So much the better," he answered. "I may have to speak to you about that, later on."

He paused, and the Second Mate said something to him, in an undertone.

"Yes," he said, as though in reply to what the Second had been saying. Then he spoke to me again.

"You've seen things come out of the sea, you say?" he questioned. "Now just tell me all you can remember, from the very beginning."

I set to, and told him everything in detail, commencing with the strange figure that had stepped aboard out of the sea, and continuing my yarn, up to the things that had happened in that very watch.

I stuck well to solid facts; and now and then he and the Second Mate would look at one another, and nod. At the end, he turned to me with an abrupt gesture.

"You still hold, then, that you saw a ship the other morning, when I sent you from the wheel?" he asked.

"Yes, Sir," I said. "I most certainly do."

"But you knew there wasn't any!" he said.

"Yes, Sir," I replied, in an apologetic tone. "There was; and, if you will let me, I believe that I can explain it a bit."

"Well," he said, "go on."

Now that I knew he was willing to listen to me in a serious manner all my funk of telling him had gone, and I went ahead and told him my ideas about the mist, and the thing it seemed to have ushered, you know. I finished up, by telling him how Tammy had worried me to come and tell what I knew.

"He thought then, Sir," I went on, "that you might wish to put into the nearest port; but I told him that I didn't think you could, even if you wanted to."

"How's that?" he asked, profoundly interested.

"Well, Sir," I replied. "If we're unable to see other vessels, we shouldn't be able to see the land. You'd be piling the ship up, without ever seeing where you were putting her."

This view of the matter affected the Old Man in an extraordinary manner; as it did, I believe, the Second Mate. And neither spoke for a moment. Then the Skipper burst out.

"By Gad! Jessop," he said. "If you're right, the Lord have mercy on us."

He thought for a couple of seconds. Then he spoke again, and I could see that he was pretty well twisted up.

"My God! . . . if you're right!"

The Second Mate spoke.

"The men mustn't know, Sir," he warned him. "It'd be a mess if they did!"

"Yes," said the Old Man.

He spoke to me.

"Remember that, Jessop," he said. "Whatever you do, don't go yarning about this, forrard."

"No, Sir," I replied.

"And you too, boy," said the Skipper. "Keep your tongue between your teeth. We're in a bad enough mess, without your making it worse. Do you hear?"

"Yes, Sir," answered Tammy.

The Old Man turned to me again.

"These things, or creatures that you say come out of the sea," he said. "You've never seen them, except after nightfall?" he asked.

"No, Sir," I replied. "Never."

He turned to the Second Mate.

"So far as I can make out, Mr. Tulipson," he remarked, "the danger seems to be only at night."

"It's always been at night, Sir," the Second answered.

The Old Man nodded.

"Have you anything to propose, Mr. Tulipson?" he asked.

"Well, Sir," replied the Second Mate. "I think you ought to have her snugged down every night, before dark!"

He spoke with considerable emphasis. Then he glanced aloft, and jerked his head in the direction of the unfurled t'gallants.

"It's a damned good thing, Sir," he said, "that it didn't come on to blow any harder."

The Old Man nodded again.

"Yes," he remarked. "We shall have to do it; but God knows when we'll get home!"

"Better late than not at all," I heard the Second mutter, under his breath.

Out loud, he said:

"And the lights, Sir?"

"Yes," said the Old Man. "I will have lamps in the rigging every night, after dark."

"Very good, Sir," assented the Second. Then he turned to us.

"It's getting daylight, Jessop," he remarked, with a glance at the sky. "You'd better take Tammy with you, and shove those lamps back again into the locker."

"Aye, Aye, Sir," I said, and went down off the poop with Tammy.

When eight bells went, at four o'clock, and the other watch came on deck to relieve us, it had been broad daylight for some time. Before we went below, the Second Mate had the three t'gallants set; and now that it was light, we were pretty curious to have a look aloft, especially up the fore; and Tom, who had been up to overhaul the gear, was questioned a lot, when he came down, as to whether there were any signs of anything queer up there. But he told us there was nothing unusual to be seen.

At eight o'clock, when we came on deck for the eight to twelve watch, I saw the Sailmaker coming forrard along the deck, from the Second Mate's old berth. He had his rule in his hand, and I knew he had been measuring the poor beggars in there, for their burial outfit. From breakfast time until near noon, he worked, shaping out three canvas wrappers from some old sailcloth. Then, with the aid of the Second Mate and one of the hands, he brought out the three dead chaps on to the after hatch, and there sewed them up, with a few lumps of holy stone at their feet. He was just finishing when eight bells went, and I heard the Old Man tell the Second Mate to call all hands aft for the burial. This was done, and one of the gangways unshipped.

We had no decent grating big enough, so they had to get off one of the hatches, and use it instead. The wind had died away during the morning, and the sea was almost a calm—the ship lifting ever so slightly to an occasional glassy heave. The only sounds that struck on the ear were the soft, slow rustle and occasional shiver of the sails, and the continuous and monotonous creak, creak of the spars and gear at the gentle movements of the vessel. And it was in this solemn half-quietness that the Skipper read the burial service.

They had put the Dutchman first upon the hatch (I could tell him by his stumpiness), and when at last the Old Man gave the signal, the Second Mate tilted his end, and he slid off, and down into the dark.

"Poor old Dutchie," I heard one of the men say, and I fancy we all felt a bit like that.

Then they lifted Jacobs on to the hatch, and when he had gone, Jock. When Jock was lifted, a sort of sudden shiver ran through the crowd. He had been a favourite in a quiet way, and I know I felt, all at once, just a bit queer. I was standing by the rail, upon the after bollard, and Tammy was next to me; while Plummer stood a little behind. As the

BURIAL OF RUDLAON.

Second Mate tilted the hatch for the last time, a little, hoarse chorus broke from the men:

"S'long, Jock! So long, Jock!"

And then, at the sudden plunge, they rushed to the side to see the last of him as he went downwards. Even the Second Mate was not able to resist this universal feeling, and he, too, peered over. From where I had been standing, I had been able to see the body take the water, and now, for a brief couple of seconds, I saw the white of the canvas, blurred by the blue of the water, dwindle and dwindle in the extreme depth. Abruptly, as I stared, it disappeared—too abruptly, it seemed to me.

"Gone!" I heard several voices say, and then our watch began to go slowly forrard, while one or two of the other, started to replace the hatch.

Tammy pointed, and nudged me.

"See, Jessop," he said. "What is it?"

"What?" I asked.

"That queer shadow," he replied. "Look!"

And then I saw what he meant. It was something big and shadowy, that appeared to be growing clearer. It occupied the exact place—so it seemed to me—in which Jock had disappeared.

"Look at it!" said Tammy, again. "It's getting bigger!"

He was pretty excited, and so was I.

I was peering down. The thing seemed to be rising out of the depths. It was taking shape. As I realized what the shape was, a queer, cold funk took me.

"See," said Tammy. "It's just like the shadow of a ship!"

And it was. The shadow of a ship rising out of the unexplored immensity beneath our keel. Plummer, who had not yet gone forrard, caught Tammy's last remark, and glanced over.

"What's 'e mean?" he asked.

"That!" replied Tammy, and pointed.

I jabbed my elbow into his ribs; but it was too late. Plummer had seen. Curiously enough, though, he seemed to think nothing of it.

"That ain't nothin', 'cept ther shadder er ther ship," he said.

Tammy, after my hint, let it go at that. But when Plummer had gone forrard with the others, I told him not to go telling everything round the decks, like that.

"We've got to be thundering careful!" I remarked. "You know what the Old Man said, last watch!"

"Yes," said Tammy. "I wasn't thinking; I'll be careful next time."

A little way from me the Second Mate was still staring down into the water. I turned, and spoke to him.

"What do you make it out to be, Sir?" I asked.

"God knows!" he said, with a quick glance round to see whether any of the men were about.

He got down from the rail, and turned to go up on to the poop. At the top of the ladder, he leaned over the break.

"You may as well ship that gangway, you two," he told us. "And mind, Jessop, keep your mouth shut about this."

"Aye, Aye, Sir," I answered.

"And you too, youngster!" he added and went aft along the poop.

Tammy and I were busy with the gangway when the Second came back. He had brought the Skipper.

"Right under the gangway, Sir," I heard the Second say, and he pointed down into the water.

For a little while, the Old Man stared. Then I heard him speak.

"I don't see anything," he said.

At that, the Second Mate bent more forward and peered down. So did I; but the thing, whatever it was, had gone completely.

"It's gone, Sir," said the Second. "It was there right enough when I came for you."

About a minute later, having finished shipping the gangway, I was going forrard, when the Second's voice called me back.

"Tell the Captain what it was you saw just now," he said, in a low voice.

"I can't say exactly, Sir," I replied. "But it seemed to me like the shadow of a ship, rising up through the water."

"There, Sir," remarked the Second Mate to the Old Man. "Just what I told you."

The Skipper stared at me.

"You're quite sure?" he asked.

"Yes, Sir," I answered. "Tammy saw it, too."

I waited a minute. Then they turned to go aft. The Second was saying something.

"Can I go, Sir?" I asked.

"Yes, that will do, Jessop," he said, over his shoulder. But the Old Man came back to the break, and spoke to me.

"Remember, not a word of this forrard!" he said.

"No Sir," I replied, and he went back to the Second Mate; while I walked forrard to the fo'cas'le to get something to eat.

"Your whack's in the kettle, Jessop," said Tom, as I stepped in over the washboard. "An' I got your lime juice in a pannikin."

"Thanks," I said, and sat down.

As I stowed away my grub, I took no notice of the chatter of the others. I was too stuffed with my own thoughts. That shadow of a vessel rising, you know, out of the profound deeps, had impressed me tremendously. It had not been imagination. Three of us had seen it—really four; for Plummer distinctly saw it; though he failed to recognize it as anything extraordinary.

As you can understand, I thought a lot about this shadow of a vessel. But, I am sure, for a time, my ideas must just have gone in an everlasting, blind circle. And then I got another thought; for I got thinking of the figures I had seen aloft in the early morning; and I began to imagine fresh things. You see, that first thing that had come up over the side, had come *out of the sea.* And it had gone back. And now there was this shadow vessel-thing—ghost ship I called it. It was a damned good name, too. And the dark, noiseless men . . . I thought a lot on these lines. Unconsciously, I put a question to myself, aloud:

"Were they the crew?"

"Eh?" said Jaskett, who was on the next chest.

I took hold of myself, as it were, and glanced at him, in an apparently careless manner.

"Did I speak?" I asked.

"Yes, mate," he replied, eyeing me, curiously. "Yer said sumthin' about a crew."

"I must have been dreaming," I said; and rose up to put away my plate.

At four o'clock, when again we went on deck, the Second Mate told me to go on with a paunch mat I was making; while Tammy, he sent to get out his sinnet. I had the mat slug on the fore side of the mainmast, between it and the after end of the house; and, in a few minutes, Tammy brought his sinnet and yarns to the mast, and made fast to one of the pins.

"What do you think it was, Jessop?" he asked, abruptly, after a short silence.

I looked at him.

"What do you think?" I replied.

"I don't know what to think," he said. "But I've a feeling that it's something to do with all the rest," and he indicated aloft, with his head.

"I've been thinking, too," I remarked.

"That it is?" he inquired.

"Yes," I answered, and told him how the idea had come to me at my dinner, that the strange men-shadows which came aboard, might come from that indistinct vessel we had seen down in the sea.

"Good Lord!" he exclaimed, as he got my meaning. And then for a little, he stood and thought.

"That's where they live, you mean?" he said, at last, and paused again.

"Well," I replied. "It can't be the sort of existence *we* should call life."

He nodded, doubtfully.

"No," he said, and was silent again.

Presently, he put out an idea that had come to him.

"You *think*, then, that that—vessel has been with us for some time, if we'd only known?" he asked.

"All along," I replied. "I mean ever since these things started."

"Supposing there are others," he said, suddenly.

I looked at him.

"If there are," I said. "You can pray to God that they won't stumble across us. It strikes me that whether they're ghosts, or not ghosts, they're blood-gutted pirates.

"It seems horrible," he said solemnly, "to be talking seriously like this, about—you know, about such things."

"I've tried to stop thinking that way," I told him. "I've felt I should go cracked, if I didn't. There's damned queer things happen at sea, I know; but this isn't one of them."

"It seems so strange and unreal, one moment, doesn't it?" he said. "And the next, you *know* it's really true, and you can't understand why you didn't always know. And yet they'd never believe, if you told them ashore about it."

"They'd believe, if they'd been in this packet in the middle watch this morning," I said.

"Besides," I went on. "They don't understand. We didn't . . . I shall always feel different now, when I read that some packet hasn't been heard of."

Tammy stared at me.

"I've heard some of the old shellbacks talking about things," he said. "But I never took them really seriously."

"Well," I said. "I guess we'll have to take this seriously. I wish to God we were home!"

"My God! so do I," he said.

For a good while after that, we both worked on in silence; but, presently, he went off on another tack.

"Do you think we'll really shorten her down every night before it gets dark?" he asked.

"Certainly," I replied. "They'll never get the men to go aloft at night, after what's happened."

"But, but—supposing they *ordered* us aloft—" he began.

"Would you go?" I interrupted.

"No!" he said, emphatically. "I'd jolly well be put in irons first!"

"That settles it, then," I replied. "You wouldn't go, nor would any one else."

At this moment the Second Mate came along.

"Shove that mat and that sinnet away, you two," he said. "Then get your brooms and clear up."

"Aye, Aye, Sir," we said, and he went on forrard.

"Jump on the house, Tammy," I said. "And let go the other end of this rope, will you?"

"Right" he said, and did as I had asked him. When he came back, I got him to give me a hand to roll up the mat, which was a very large one.

"I'll finish stopping it," I said. "You go and put your sinnet away."

"Wait a minute," he replied, and gathered up a double handful of shakins from the deck, under where I had been working. Then he ran to the side.

"Here!" I said. "Don't go dumping those. They'll only float, and the Second Mate or the Skipper will be sure to spot them."

"Come here, Jessop!" he interrupted, in a low voice, and taking no notice of what I had been saying.

I got up off the hatch, where I was kneeling. He was staring over the side.

"What's up?" I asked.

"For God's sake, hurry!" he said, and I ran, and jumped on to the spar, alongside of him.

"Look!" he said, and pointed with a handful of shakins, right down, directly beneath us.

Some of the shakins dropped from his hand, and blurred the water, momentarily, so that I could not see. Then, as the ripples cleared away, I saw what he meant.

"Two of them!" he said, in a voice that was scarcely above a whisper. "And there's another out there," and he pointed again with the handful of shakins.

"There's another a little further aft," I muttered.

"Where?—where?" he asked.

"There," I said, and pointed.

"That's four," he whispered. "Four of them!"

I said nothing; but continued to stare. They appeared to me to be a great way down in the sea, and quite motionless. Yet, though their outlines were somewhat blurred and indistinct, there was no mistaking that they were very like exact, though shadowy, representations of vessels. For some minutes we watched them, without speaking.

At last Tammy spoke.

"They're real, right enough," he said, in a low voice.

"I don't know," I answered.

"I mean we weren't mistaken this morning," he said.

"No," I replied. "I never thought we were."

Away forrard, I heard the Second Mate, returning aft. He came nearer, and saw us.

"What's up now, you two?" he called, sharply. "This isn't clearing up!"

I put out my hand to warn him not to shout, and draw the attention of the rest of the men.

He took several steps toward me.

"What is it? What is it?" he said, with a certain irritability; but in a lower voice.

"You'd better take a look over the side, Sir," I replied.

My tone must have given him an inkling that we had discovered something fresh; for, at my words, he made one spring, and stood on the spar, alongside of me.

"Look, Sir," said Tammy. "There's four of them."

The Second Mate glanced down, saw something and bent sharply forward.

"My God!" I heard him mutter, under his breath. ☾

chapter 2

Among the Malay Pirates

BY G. A. HENTY

The party landed at the village the next morning, but found it entirely deserted.

"It is most important that we should take a prisoner, Ferguson," the captain said, as he and the first lieutenant paced up and down the quarterdeck; "we must catch the two prahus [pirate craft] if we can. At present we don't know whether they have gone up or down the river, and it would be absolutely useless for us to wait until we get some clue to their whereabouts. After we have finished with them, we will go up the other branch, and try to find the two we know to be up there. I should not like to leave our work unfinished."

"Certainly not, sir. I am afraid, though, it is of no use landing to try to get hold of a prisoner. No doubt the woods are full of them. There are the townspeople and those who came to help them; and though many of those who tried to swim ashore from the sunken boats may have been taken by the alligators, still the greater portion must have landed all right."

"I should think, Mr. Ferguson, that it would be a good plan to send a party of twenty men on shore after nightfall and to distribute them, two men to a hut. Possibly two or three of the Malays may come down to the village before morning, either to fetch valuables they may have left behind, or to see whether we are still here. They may come tonight, or they may come some time tomorrow, crawling through the plantations behind the houses. At any rate, I will wait here a day or two on the chance."

"Whom shall I send with the men, sir?"

"You had better send Parkhurst and Balderson; they will have more authority among the men than the younger midshipmen. The men better take three days' cooked provisions on shore and ten small kegs of water, one for each hut. I will give Parkhurst his instructions before he lands."

"Now, Mr. Parkhurst," he said, when the boat was lowered soon after dark, "you must bear in mind that the greatest vigilance will be necessary. Choose ten huts close together. One man in each hut must be always awake; there must be no talking above a whisper; and during the daytime no one must leave his hut on any account whatever. After nightfall you and Mr. Balderson will move from hut to hut, to see that a vigilant watch is kept. You must, of course, take watch and watch, night and day. You must remember that not only is it most important that a native should be captured, but you must be on your guard against an attack on yourselves. It is quite conceivable that a party may come down to see if there are any of us in the village.

"In case of attack, you must gather in one hut, and fire three shots as a signal to us; a musket shot will be fired in return. When you hear it, every man must throw himself down, for the guns will be already loaded with grape, and I shall fire a broadside towards the spot where I have heard your signal.

"As soon as the broadside is fired, make down to the shore, occupy a house close to the water, and keep the Malays off till the boats come ashore to fetch you off. Your crew has been very carefully picked. I have consulted the warrant officers, and they have selected the most taciturn men in the ship. There is to be no smoking; of course the men can chew as much as they like; but the smell of tobacco smoke would at once deter any native from entering a hut. If a Malay should come in and try to escape, he must be fired on as he runs away; but the men are to aim at his legs."

The instructions were carried out. A small hole was bored in the back of each of the huts, so that a constant watch could be kept up unseen by the closest observer in the forest, a hundred yards behind. The night passed off quietly, as did the next day. The men slept and watched by turns. On the afternoon of the second day, a native was seen moving cautiously from tree to tree along the edge of the forest. As soon as it was dark, Dick, whose watch it was, crawled cautiously from hut to hut.

"That fellow we saw today may come at any moment," he said. "If one of you see him coming, the other must place himself close to the door, and if he enters, throw himself upon him and hold his arms tightly till the others come up to help. Keep your rope handy to twist round him, and remember these fellows are as slippery as eels."

Having made the round, he returned to the hut in the center of the others that he and Harry occupied. Half an hour later, they heard a sudden outcry from the hut next to them, and rushing in, found the two men there struggling with a Malay. With their aid he was speedily bound; then the men were called from the other huts, and the whole party ran down to the water's edge, where Harry hailed the ship. A boat put off at once, and they were taken on board. The prisoner was led to the captain's cabin, and there examined through the medium of the interpreter. He refused to answer any questions until, by the captain's orders, he was taken on deck again and a noose placed round his neck, and the interpreter told him that, unless he spoke, he was to be hauled up to the yard's arm. The man was still silent.

"Tighten the strain very gradually," the captain said to the sailors holding the other end of the rope. "Raise him two or three feet above the deck, and then, when the doctor holds up his hand, lower him at once again."

This was done. The man, though half strangled, was still conscious, and on the noose being loosened, and Soh Hay saying that, unless he spoke, he would be again run up, he said, as soon as he got his breath, that he would answer any question. On being taken to the cabin, he said that the prahus had gone down the river, and had ascended the other arm. They had only gone a few miles above the town, for one had been so injured that there had been difficulty in keeping her afloat, and it was necessary to run her into a creek in order to repair her before going up farther.

Half an hour later steam was up, and before morning the *Serpent* lay off the mouth of the creek which the Malay pointed out as the one that the prahu had entered. The second officer was this time placed in command of the boats, he himself going in the launch, the third officer took the first cutter, the two midshipmen the second. No time was lost in making preparations, for it was desirable to capture the prahu before she was aware that the *Serpent* had left her position in the other river. For a mile the boats rowed up the creek, which narrowed until they were obliged to go in single file. It widened suddenly, and as the launch dashed through, a shower of balls tore up the water round her; while at the same moment a great tree fell across the creek, completely barring their retreat, and narrowly shaving the stern of the midshipmen's boat, which was the last in the line. Fortunately the launch had escaped serious injury, and with a shout of "Treachery," Lieutenant Hopkins drew his pistol to put a ball through the head of their guide, but as he did so, the man sprang overboard and dived towards the shore.

"Row, men; we have all our work cut out for us. There are three prahus ahead; steer for the center one, coxswain."

With a cheer the men bent to their oars, and dashed at the prahu which, as was evident by patches of plank freshly fastened to her side, was one of those that had before escaped them.

"Follow me," the lieutenant shouted to the boat behind, "we must take them one by one." The three boats dashed at the pirate craft, which was crowded with men, regardless of the fire from the other two vessels. The launch steered for her stem, the first cutter for her bow, while the midshipmen swept round her, and boarded her on the opposite side. A furious contest took place on her deck, the Malays being so confused by being assailed at three points simultaneously that the midshipmen's party were enabled to gain a footing with but very slight resistance. The shouts of the Malays near them brought many running from the other points, and the parties there gained a footing with comparatively little loss. Then a desperate struggle began; but the Malays were unable to

withstand the furious attack of the British, and ere long began to leap overboard and swim to the other craft, which were both coming to their aid.

The launch's gun had not been fired, and, calling to Dick, Harry leaped down into the boat. The two midshipmen trained the gun upon the nearest prahu, and aiming at the waterline, fired it when the craft was within twenty feet of them. A moment later its impetus brought it against the side of the launch, which was crushed like an eggshell between it and the captured prahu, the two midshipmen springing on board just in time. It was the Malays turn to board now, that of the British to prevent them; the musketry of the sailors and marines for a time kept the enemy off, but they strove desperately to gain a footing on board, until a loud cry was heard, and the craft into which the midshipmen had fired sank suddenly, and a loud cheer broke from the British.

The two midshipmen were engaged with the other pirate, from whom a cry of dismay arose at seeing the disappearance of their friends.

"Now, lads, follow me," Harry shouted as the Malays strove to push their craft away. Followed by a dozen sailors, they leaped onto her deck; but the efforts of the Malays succeeded in thrusting the vessels apart. In vain the midshipmen and their followers fought desperately. Harry was felled by a blow with a war club, Dick cut down with a kris; half the seamen were killed, the others jumped overboard and swam back to their vessel. Lieutenant Hopkins shouted to the men to take to the boats, and the two cutters were speedily manned. One, however, was in a sinking condition; but Lieutenant Hopkins with the other started in pursuit of the prahu, whose crew had already got their oars out, and in spite of the efforts of the sailors, soon left them behind. Pursuit was evidently hopeless, and reluctantly the lieutenant ordered the men to row back. On returning to the scene of combat, they saw sunk near the bank the fourth of the prahus. "The spy was so far right," the second lieutenant muttered—"this fellow did sink; now we must see that she does no more mischief." He brought the captured prahu alongside the others, whose decks were but a foot or two below the water, and fired several shots through their bottoms. Then he set the captured craft on fire and took to the boats, which with great difficulty forced their way under the fallen tree and rowed back to the ship.

The third lieutenant had been shot dead, twelve men had been killed, ten of the midshipmen's party were missing, and of the rest but few had escaped without wounds more or less serious.

Harry was the first to recover his senses, being roughly brought to by a bucket of water being dashed over him. He looked round the deck. Of those who had sprung on board with him, none were visible save Dick Balderson, who was lying near him, with a cloth tightly bound round his shoulder.

As he rose into a sitting position a murmur of satisfaction broke from some Malays standing near. It was some time before he could rally his senses.

"I suppose," he thought at last, "they are either keeping us for torture or as hostages. The rajah may have given orders that any officers captured were to be spared and brought to him. I don't know what his expectations are," he muttered to himself, "but if he expects to be reinstated as rajah, and perhaps compensated for the loss of his palace, he is likely to be mistaken; and in that case it will go mighty hard with us, for there is no shadow of doubt that he is a savage and cruel brute."

He had now shaken off the numbness caused by the blow that he had received, and he managed to stagger to where Dick was lying, and knelt beside him and begged the Malays to bring water. They had evidently received orders to do all they could to revive the two young officers, and one at once brought half a gourd full. Harry had already assured himself that his friend's heart still beat. He began by pouring some water between his lips. It was not necessary to pour any over his head, for he had already received the same treatment as himself.

"Dick, old chap," he said sharply and earnestly.

The sound was evidently heard and understood, for Dick started slightly, opened his eyes and murmured, "It's not time to turn out yet?"

"You are not in your hammock, Dick; you have been wounded, and we are both prisoners in the hands of these Malays. Try and pull yourself together, but don't move; they have .put a sort of bandage round your shoulder, and I am going to try and improve it."

"What is the matter with my shoulder?" Dick murmured.

"Chopped with a kris, old man. Now I am going to turn you on your side, and then cut the sleeve off the jacket. Take another drink of water; then we will set about it."

Dick did as he was ordered, and was evidently coming back to consciousness, for he looked round, and then said, "Where are the other fellows?"

"I don't know what has become of them. I think I went down before you did. However, here we are alone. Now I am going to begin."

He cut off the sleeve of the jacket and shirt at the shoulder, ripped open the seam to the neck, first taking off the rough bandage.

"It's a nasty cut, old man," he said, "but nothing dangerous, I should say. I fancy it has gone clean through the shoulder bone, and there is no doubt that it will knit again, as Hassan's did, if they do but give you time."

He rolled the shirt sleeve into a pad, saturated it with water, and laid it on the wound.

"You see I know all about it, Dick," he said cheerily, "from having watched the doctor at work on Hassan. Now I will tear this cloth into strips."

He first placed a strip of the cloth over the shoulder, crossed it under the arm, and then took the ends of the bandage across the chest and back, and tied them under his other arm. He repeated this process with half a dozen other strips; then he placed Dick's hand upon his chest, tied some of the other strips together, and bound them tightly round the arm and body, so that no movement of the limb was possible. One of the Malay's knelt down and gave him his assistance, and nodded approvingly when he had finished; then he helped Harry raise him into a sitting position against the bulwark.

"That is better," Dick said, "as far as it goes. How was it these fellows did not kill us at once?"

"I expect the rajah has ordered that all officers who may fall into their hands are to be kept as hostages, so that he can open negotiations with the skipper. If he gets what he wants, he hands us back; if not, there is no manner of doubt that he will put us out of the way without compunction."

The men were still working at the oars, and for four hours rowed without intermission through a labyrinth of creeks. At last they stopped before a small village, tied the prahu up to a tree, and then the man who seemed to be the captain went ashore with two or three others. The lads heard a loud outburst of anger, and a voice which they recognized as that of the rajah storming and raging for some time; then the hubbub ceased. An hour later the rajah himself came on board with two or three attendants, and a man whom they recognized as speaking a certain amount of English. The rajah scowled at them, and from the manner in which he kept fingering his kris they saw that it needed a great effort on his part to abstain from killing them at once. He spoke for some time in his own language, and the interpreter translated it.

"You are dogs—you and all your countrymen. The rajah is sending a message to your captain to tell him that he must build up his palace again, pay him for the warships that he has destroyed, and provide him with a guard against his enemies until a fresh fleet has been built. If he refuses to do this, you will both be killed."

"Tell him," Harry said, "that if we are dogs, anyhow we have shown him that we can bite. As to what he says, it is for the captain to answer; but I do not think that he will grant the terms, though possibly he may consent to spare the rajah's life, and to go away with his ship, if we are sent back to him without injury."

The rajah uttered a scornful exclamation. "I have six thousand men," he said, "and I do not need to beg my life; for were there twenty ships instead of one they could never find me, and not a man who landed and tried to come through the country would return alive. I have given your captain the chance. If, at the end of three days, an answer does not come granting my command, you will be krised. Keep a strict watch upon them, Captain, and kill them at once if they try to escape."

"I will guard them safely, Rajah," the captain, who, from the rich materials of his sarong and jacket, was evidently himself a chief, said quietly; "but as to escape, where could they go? They could but wander in the jungle until they died."

By night both lads felt more themselves. They had been well supplied with food, and though Harry's head ached until, as he said, it was splitting, and Dick's wound smarted severely, they were able to discuss their position. They at once agreed that escape was impossible, and would be even were they well and strong and could manage to obtain possession of a sampan, for they would but lose themselves in the labyrinth of creeks, and would, moreover, be certain to be overtaken by the native boats that would be sent off in all directions after them.

"There is nothing to do but to wait for the captain's answer," Dick said at last.

"We know what that will be," Harry said. "He will tell the chief that it would be impossible for him to grant his commands, but that he is ready to pay a certain sum for our release; that if harm comes to us, he will make peace with the chiefs who have assisted Sehi against us, on condition of their hunting him down and sending him alive or dead to the ships. But the rascal knows that he could hide himself in these swamps for a month, and he will proceed to chop off our heads without a moment's delay. We must keep our eyes open tomorrow, and endeavor to get hold of a couple of weapons. It is a deal better to die fighting than it is to have our throats cut like sheep."

The next two days passed quietly. The lads were both a great deal better, and agreed that if—which would almost certainly not be the case— a means of escape should present itself, they would seize the chance, however hopeless it might be, for that at worst they could but be cut down in attempting it. No chance, however, presented itself. Two Malays always squatted near them, and their eyes followed every movement.

"Sometime tomorrow the messenger will return," Harry said. "It is clear to me that our only chance is to escape before morning. Those fellows will be watchful till the night is nearly over. Now, I propose that, just before the first gleam of daylight, we throw ourselves upon them suddenly, seize their krises, and cut them down, then leap on shore, and dash into the jungle. The night will be as dark as pitch, what with there being no moon and with the mist from the swamps. At any rate, we might get out of sight before the Malays knew what had happened. We could either go straight into the jungle and crawl into the thick bushes, and lie there until morning, and then make our start, or, what would, I think, be even better, take to the water, wade along under the bank till

we reach one of those sampans fifty yards away, get in, and manage to paddle it noiselessly across to the opposite side, lift the craft out of the water, and hide it among the bushes, and then be off."

"The worst of it is the alligators, Harry."

"Yes, but we must risk that. We shall have the krises, and if they seize either of us, the other must go down and try and jab his kris into the beast's eyes. I know it is a frightfully dangerous business, and the chances are one hundred to one against our succeeding; but there is just a chance, and there is no chance at all if we leave it until tomorrow. Of course, if we succeed in getting over to the other side, we must wait close to the water until daylight. We should tear ourselves to pieces if we tried to make through the jungle in the dark."

"I tell you what would give us a better chance—we might take off two or three yards of that bandage of yours, cut the strip in half, and twist it into a rope; then when those fellows doze off a little, we might throw the things round their necks, and it would be all up with them."

"But you see I have only one arm, Harry."

"Bother it! I never thought of that. Well, I might do the securing, one fellow first, and then the other. You could get close to him, and if he moves, catch up his kris and cut him down."

"Yes, I could do that. Well, anyhow, Harry, we can but try; anything is better than waiting here hour after hour for the messenger to come back with what will be our death warrant."

They agreed to keep awake by turns, and accordingly lay down as soon as it became dark, the Malays, as usual, squatting at a distance of a couple of paces each side of them. It was about two o'clock in the morning when Dick, who was awake, saw, as he supposed, one of the crew standing up a few yards away; he was not sure, for just at that moment the figure disappeared.

"What on earth could that fellow want to stand up for and lie down again? for I can swear he was not there half a minute ago. There is another farther on." He pinched himself to make sure that he was awake. Figure after figure seemed to flit along the deck and disappear. One of the guard rose and stretched his arms; put a fresh bit of some herb that he was chewing into his mouth; moved close to the prisoners to see if they were asleep; and then resumed his former position. During the time that he was on his feet, Dick noticed that the phenomenon that had so puzzled him ceased. A quarter of an hour later it began again. He touched Harry, keeping his hand on his lips as a warning to be silent. Suddenly a wild yell broke on the still air, and in an instant the deck was alive with men; and as the two Malay watchers rose to their feet, both were cut down.

There were sounds of heavy blows, screams and yells, a short and confused struggle, and the fall of heavy bodies, while from the little village there were also sounds of conflict. The midshipmen had started to their feet, half bewildered at the sudden and desperate struggle, when a hand was laid on each of their shoulders, and a voice said, "English friends, Hassan has come."

The revulsion of feeling was so great that, for a minute, neither could speak; then Dick said, "Chief, we thank you with all our hearts. Tomorrow we should have been killed."

The chief shook hands with them both warmly, having seen that mode of salutation on board ship.

"Hassan glad," he said. "Hassan watch all time; no let Sehi kill friends. Friends save Hassan's child; he save them."

Torches were now lighted. The deck was thickly encumbered with dead; for every one of the crew of the prahu had been killed.

"Sehi killed too," the chief said, "come and see." He swung himself on shore; the boys followed his example, two of the Malays helping Dick down. They went to the village, where a number of Malays were moving about; torches had been brought from the ship, and a score of these soon lit up the scene. Two of the rajah's men had been killed outside their huts, but the majority had fallen inside. The chief asked a question of one of his followers, who pointed to a hut.

This they entered, and by the light of the torches saw the rajah lying dead upon the ground. Hassan said something to one of his men, who, with a single blow, chopped off the rajah's head.

"Send to chiefs," Hassan said. "If not see, not think dead. Much afraid of him. When know he dead, not fight any more; make peace quick."

One of the men asked a question, and the lads' limited knowledge of the language was sufficient to tell them that he was asking whether they should fire the village. Hassan shook his head. "Many men," he said, waving his arm to the forest, "see fire; come fight. Plenty of fight been; no need for more." For a time he stood with them in front of the pool. A series of splashes in the water told what was going on. The prahu was being cleared of its load of dead bodies; then several men filled buckets with water, and handed them up to the deck. The boys knew that an attempt was being made to wash away the blood. The process was repeated a dozen times. While this was going on, the pool was agitated in every direction. The lads shuddered as they looked, and remembered that they had proposed to wade along the edge. The place swarmed with alligators, who scrambled and fought for the bodies thrown over, until the number was so great that all were satisfied, and the pool became comparatively quiet, although fresh monsters, guided by the smell of blood, kept arriving on the scene.

At last the chief said, "Come," and together they returned to the prahu. The morning was now breaking, and but few signs remained of the terrible conflict of the night. At the chief's order, a large basket of wine, which had been found in the rajah's hut, was brought on board, together with another, full of bananas and other fruit.

"Well," Harry said, laughing, "we little thought, when we saw the champagne handed over to the rajah, that we were going to have the serving of it."

Hassan joined them at the meal. He had been given wine regularly by the doctor, and although he had evinced no partiality for it, but had taken it simply at the doctor's orders, he now drank a little to keep the others company. In a short time the whole of the chief's followers were gathered on deck, and the boys saw that they were no more numerous than the prahu's crew, and that it was only the advantage of surprise that had enabled them to overcome so easily both those on board the prahu and the rajah's followers in the village. The oars were got out, and the prahu proceeded up the creek, in the opposite direction to which it had entered it. "Going to ship?" Harry asked, pointing forward.

Hassan shook his head. "Going home," he said. "Sent messenger sampan tell captain both safe. Sehi killed, prahu taken. Must go home. Others angry because Hassan not join. May come and fight Hassan. Ask captain bring ship up river; messenger show channel, tell how far can go, then come in boats, hold great meeting, make peace."

The lads were well satisfied. They had a longing to see Hassan's home, and, perhaps, to do some shooting; and they thought that a few days holiday before rejoining would be by no means unpleasant. They wished, however, that they had known that the sampan was leaving, so that they could have written a line to the captain, saying what had taken place, and that they could not rejoin. There was at first some splashing of the oars, for many of Hassan's men had had no prior experience except with sampans and large canoes. However, it was not long before they fell into the swing, and the boat proceeded at a rapid pace. Several times, as they went, natives appeared on the bank in considerable numbers, and receiving no answer to their hails, sent showers of lances. Harry, however, with the aid of two or three Malays, soon loaded the guns of the prahu.

"No kill," Hassan said. "We want make friends. No good kill."

Accordingly the guns were fired far over the heads of the assailants, who at once took to the bushes. After three hours rowing they entered the river, and continued their course up it until long into the night, for the rowers were as anxious as was Hassan himself to reach their village. They were numerous enough to furnish relays at the oars, and the stroke never flagged until, an hour before midnight, fires were seen burning ahead, as they turned a bend of the river. The Malays raised a yell of triumph, which was answered from the village, and in a few minutes the prahu was brought up to the bank. A crowd, composed mostly of women and children, received them with shouts of welcome and gladness. Hassan at once led the midshipmen to a large hut that had evidently been prepared in readiness for them. Piles of skins lay in two of the corners, and the lads, who were utterly worn out, threw themselves down, and were almost instantly asleep.

The sun was high when the mat at the entrance was drawn aside, and Hassan entered, followed by four of his followers. One carried a great water jar and two calabashes, with some cotton cloths and towels; the other brought fruit of several varieties, eggs, and sweetmeats, together with a large gourd full of steaming coffee.

"Hassan come again," the chief said, and left the hut with his followers. The lads poured calabashes of water over each other, and felt wonderfully refreshed by their wash, which was accomplished without damage to the floor, which was of bamboos raised two feet above the ground. When they were dressed they fell to at their breakfast, and then went out of doors. Hassan had evidently been watching for them, for he came out of his house, which was next to that which they occupied, holding his little girl's hand. She at once ran up to them, saluting them by their names.

"Bahi very glad to see you," she said, "very glad to see good, kind officers." The child had picked up, during her month on board the ship, a great deal of English, from her constant communication with the officers and crew.

"Bad men wound Dick," she went on pitifully. "Wicked men to hurt him."

"Bahi, will you tell your father how much we are obliged to him for having come to our rescue. We should have been killed if he had not come."

The child translated the sentence. The chief smiled.

"Tell them," he said, "that Hassan is glad to have been able to pay back a little of the obligation he was under to them. Besides, Sehi Pandash was my enemy. Good thing to help friends and kill enemy at the same time. Tell them that Hassan does not want thanks; they did not like him to thank them for saving you."

The child translated this with some difficulty. Then he led the midshipmen round the village, and showed them the strong palisade that had evidently just been erected, and explained, through the child, that it had only been built before he left, as but fifteen men were available for guarding the place in his absence.

The next four days were spent in shooting expeditions, and although they met with no wild beasts, they secured a large number of bird skins for the doctor. On the fifth day a native ran in and said that boats with white men were coming. The midshipmen ran down to the bank, and saw the ship's two cutters and a gig approaching. The captain himself was in the stern of the latter, and the doctor was sitting beside him. A minute or two later they were shaking hands with the officers, and saying a few words to the men, who were evidently delighted to see them again. Just as the greetings were over, Hassan, in a rich silk sarong and jacket, came down towards them. He was leading his little daughter, and six Malays followed them.

"Welcome, Captain," he said gravely. "Hassan very glad to see you. All come right now."

"Thank you, chief. We have learned from your messenger how gallantly you have rescued my two officers, and put an end to our troubles by killing the Rajah Sehi, and capturing the last of the piratical craft."

This was too much for Hassan, and had to be translated by Soh Hay. Since the chief's return, a number of his men had been occupied in constructing bamboo huts for the use of the captain, officers, and men, also a large hall to be used for councils and meetings; and to this he now led the captain and his officers. When they were seated, he made a speech of welcome, saying what gladness it was to him to see there those who had been so kind to him. Had he known when they would arrive, food would have been ready for them; and he assured them that, however long they might stay, they would be most heartily welcome, and that there should be no lack of provisions. They had done an immense service to him, and to all the other chiefs on the river, by breaking up the power of one who preyed upon all his neighbors, and was a scourge to trade. As there were still several bottles of the rajah's wine left, champagne was now handed round.

"It makes my heart glad to see you, Doctor," the chief said. "See, I am as strong and as well as ever. Had it not been for you, my arm might now have been useless, and my ribs have grown through the flesh."

"I don't think it would have been as bad as that," the doctor replied, "but there is no doubt that it was fortunate that you were able to receive surgical treatment so soon after the accident. And it has been fortunate for us, too, especially for our young friends here."

Conversation became general now, and the interpreter was kept hard at work, and Bahi divided her attention between the officers and the men, flitting in and out of the hall, and chattering away to the sailors and marines who were breakfasting outside on the stores they had brought up, supplemented by a bountiful supply of fruit that grew in abundance round the village. It was not long before a meal was served to the officers, fowl having been hastily killed as soon as the boats were seen approaching; several jungle fowl had been brought in that morning; plaintains and rice were boiled, and cakes baked. Tea was forthcoming from the boats' stores, and a hearty meal was eaten.

After the meal was concluded, the captain said to the chief:

"Now, Hassan, we want to know how it was that you arrived at the nick of time to save my officers' lives."

"I had been watching for some days," the chief said quietly. "When I heard that many chiefs had joined Sehi Pandash, I said, 'I must go and help my white brothers,' but I dared not take many men away from here, and as I had to hide, the fewer there were with me the better; so I came down into the forest near Sehi's town, and found the wood full of men. We had come down in sampans, so that I could send off messengers as might be required. One of these I sent down to you, to warn you to be prepared for an attack. Other messengers I had sent before from here; but they must have been caught and killed, for I had been watched closely when they found that I would not join against you.

"When my last messenger returned, I was glad; I knew that you would be on your guard, and would not be caught treacherously. Two of my men were in the town when they began to fire on the ship, and I saw the town destroyed, and followed Sehi to the place where the six prahus were lying, and crossed the creek, and lay down in the woods near the village on the other side; for I thought that something might happen. One of my men went down in the night, and brought me news that the ship was gone. As my messenger had told me that you had questioned him as to the other entrance to the creek, I felt sure that you had gone there; so I was not surprised when, just before daybreak, two guns were fired. We saw the fight, the sinking of two of their vessels, and the attack by the water pirates, and by the men of the rajah and the chiefs with him, and I feared greatly that my friends would be overpowered.

"I sent one of my men down to the mouth of the creek, to tell you how much aid was wanted; but he saw the ship steaming up as he went, and so came back to me. Then we heard the ship's great guns begin to fire, and soon all was quiet where the fight had been going on. Then I saw the other four boats start. One of them sank before she was out of sight, and I soon heard that your ship had sunk another, and that two had got away. It was not for another two days that I learned where they were, and then I heard that they had gone into a creek twenty miles away; there one had sunk, and the other had been joined by the two prahus that had been far up the river; and I also learned that one of Sehi's men had gone into the village and let himself be captured, so that he might guide the ship's boats to the place where, as they thought, they would find but one prahu, while three would be waiting for them. I was not sure where the exact place was, for there are many creeks, but, with

one of my men, I rowed in a sampan all night, in hopes to arrive in time to warn the boats; but it was not till I heard the firing that I knew exactly where they were.

"When I got there the fighting was over, and but one prahu had escaped, and I learned from the men who had swum ashore from those that had been sunk that one of the English boats had been destroyed, and many men killed, but that two boats had gone down the creek again. It was also said that the white officers and sailors had boarded the boat that had escaped, and had been all killed. I thought it best to follow the prahu, so that I could send word to you where she was to be found. As there were many passages, it was difficult to find her, and I should have lost her altogether had I not heard where Sehi was hiding, and guessed that she would go there. It was late when I arrived at the village. There one of my men learned that two young officers, who had been wounded, had been brought there, and that Sehi was sending word to you that, unless you gave him the conditions he asked, they would be put to death.

"I did not know whether to send down to you, or to send up the river for help; but I thought the last was best, for if you came in boats, then Sehi's men would hear you, and the officers would be killed; so I sent off my man with the sampan. I told him that he must not stop until he got here. He must tell them that all my men, except fifty old ones who were to guard the village, were to start in their canoes, and paddle their hardest till they came within half a mile of the village, and he was to come back with them to guide them, and I was to meet them. As the prahus that had been up there were destroyed, the river was safe for them to descend. I said that they must be at the point I named last evening. They were two hours late, though they had paddled their hardest. As soon as they disembarked I led them to the spot, and the rest was easy. I knew that the prisoners who had been taken were my two friends, for I saw them on the deck of the prahu; and glad indeed I was to be able to pay my debt to them."

"You have paid it indeed most nobly, Hassan," the captain said, holding out his hand, and grasping that of the chief, when, sentence by sentence, the story was translated to him. "Little did we think, when you were brought on board the *Serpent*, that your friendship would turn out of such value to us."

There was now some discussion as to the proposed meeting of chiefs; and half an hour after, a dozen small canoes started with invitations to the various chiefs to meet the captain at Hassan's campong, with assurances that he was ready to overlook their share in the attack on the ship, and be on friendly terms with them, and that the safety of each who attended was guaranteed, whether he was willing to be on good terms with the English or not. Four days later, the meeting took place in the newly erected hall. Ten or twelve of the chiefs attended; others, who had taken a leading part as Sehi's allies, did not venture to come themselves, but sent messages with assurances of their desire to be on friendly terms. A good deal of ceremony was observed. The marines and blue-jackets were drawn up in line before the hall, which was decorated with green boughs; a Union jack waved from a pole in front of it.

The chiefs were introduced by Hassan to the captain. The former then addressed them, rehearsing the service that the English had done to them by destroying the power of the tyrant who had long been a scourge to his neighbors, and who intended, without doubt, to become master of the whole district. As a proof of the goodwill of the English towards the Malays, he related how the two English officers had leaped into the water to save his child, and how kindly he himself had been treated. Then the captain addressed them through the interpreter. He told them that he had only been sent up the river by the Governor in accordance with an invitation from Sehi, of whose conduct he was igno-rant, to undertake the protectorate of his district; and that, on learning his true character, he at once reported to the Governor that the rajah was not a proper person to receive protection, as not only did he prevent trade and harass his neighbors, but was the owner of a number of pirat-ical craft, that often descended the river and plundered the coast.

"England," he went on, "has no desire whatever to take under her protection any who do not earnestly desire it, and who are not willing, in return, to promote trade, and keep peace with their neighbors; nor can she make separate arrangements with minor chiefs. It was only because she understood that Sehi ruled over a considerable extent of territory, and was all powerful in this part, that his request was listened to.

"I shall shortly return down the river," he said, "and have no thought or intention of interfering in any way with matters here. I wish to leave on good terms with you all, and to explain to you that it is to your interest to do all in your power to further trade, both by sending down your products to the coast, and by throwing no hindrance in the way of the products of the highlands coming down the river, charging, at the utmost, a very small toll upon each boat that passes up and down. It is the interest of all of you, of the people of the hills, and of ourselves, that trade should increase. Now that Sehi is dead and his people altogether dispersed and all his piratical craft destroyed, with the exception of the one captured by Hassan, there is no obstruction to trade, and you are free from the fear that he would one day eat you up.

"Be assured that there is nothing to be feared from us. You all know how greatly the States protected by us have flourished and how wealthy their rajahs have become from the increase of cultivation and the cessation of tribal wars. If in the future all the chiefs of this district should desire to place themselves under English protection, their request will be considered; but there is not the slightest desire on the part of the Governor to assume further responsibility, and he will be well satisfied indeed to know that there is peace among the river tribes, security for trade, and a large increase in the cultivation of the country and in its prosperity."

There was a general expression of satisfaction and relief upon the face of the chiefs, as, sentence by sentence, the speech was translated to them; and, one by one, they rose after its conclusion, and expressed their hearty concurrence with what had been said.

"We know," one of them said, "that these wars do much harm; but if we quarrel, or if one ill treats another, or encourages his slaves to leave him, or ravages his plantations, what are we to do?"

"That I have thought of," the captain said. "I have spoken with the chief Hassan, and he has agreed to remove with his people to the spot where Sehi's town stood. There, doubtless, he will be joined by Sehi's former subjects, who cannot but be well pleased at being rid of a tyrant who had forcibly taken them under his rule. He will retain the prahu that he has taken, and will use it to keep the two rivers free of robbers, but in no other respect will he interfere with his neighbors. His desire is to cultivate the land, clear away the forest, and encourage his people to raise products that he can send down the river to trade with us. He will occupy the territory only as far as the creek that runs between the two rivers. I propose that all of you shall come to an agreement to submit any disputes that may arise between you to his decision, swearing to accept his judgment, whichever way it may go. This is the way in which the disputes are settled in our country. Both sides go before a judge, and he hears their statements and those of their witnesses, and then decides the case; and even the government of the country is bound by his decision. I don't wish you to give me any reply as to this. I make the suggestion solely for your own good, and it is for you to talk it over among yourselves, and see if you cannot all come to an agreement that will put a stop to the senseless wars, and enable your people to cultivate the land in peace, and to obtain all the comforts that arise from trade."

A boat had been sent down to the ship, and this returned with a number of the articles that had been put on board her as presents for Sehi and other chiefs. These were now distributed. A feast was then held, and the next morning the chiefs started for their homes, highly gratified with the result of the meeting. On the following day, the British boats also took their way down the river, followed by the prahu, with a considerable number of Hassan's men, who were to clear away the ruins of Sehi's campong, to bury the dead still lying among them, and to erect huts for the whole community. The *Serpent* remained for a week opposite the town; a considerable quantity of flour, sugar, and other useful stores being landed for the use of Hassan's people. Dr. Horsley was gladdened by Hassan's promise that his people should be instructed to search for specimens of birds, butterflies, and other insects, and that these should be treated according to his instructions, and should be from time to time, as occasion offered, sent down to him in large cases to Singapore. To the two midshipmen the chief gave krises of the finest temper.

"I have no presents to give you worthy of your acceptance," he said, "but you know that I shall never forget you, and always regard you as brothers. I intend to send twelve of my young men down to Penang, there to live for three years and learn useful trades from your people. The doctor has advised me also to send Bahi, and has promised to find a comfortable home for her, where she will learn to read and write your language and many other useful things. It is hard to part with her; but it is for her good and that of her people. If you will write to me sometimes, she will read the letters to me and write letters to you in return, so that, though we are away from each other, we may know that neither of us has forgotten the other."

Bahi and twelve young Malays were taken to Penang in the *Serpent*, where the doctor found a comfortable home for her with some friends of his, to whom payment for her board and schooling was to be paid by Hassan in blocks of tin, which he would obtain from boats coming down from the hills in exchange for other articles of trade. The Malays were placed with men of their own race belonging to the protected States, and settled as carpenters, smiths, and other tradesmen in Penang. Three years later, they and Bahi were all taken back in the *Serpent* to their home.

The river was acquiring considerable importance from the great increase of trade. They found Hassan's town far more extensive and flourishing than it had been in the time of its predecessor. The forest had been cleared for a considerable distance round it; the former inhabitants had returned; tobacco, sugar canes, cotton, pepper, and other crops whose products were useful for trade purposes, were largely cultivated, while orchards of fruit trees had been extensively planted. Hassan reported that tribal wars had almost ceased, and that disputes were in almost all cases brought for his arbitration. Owing to the abolition of all oppressive tolls, trade from the interior had very largely increased, a great deal of tin, together with spices and other products, now finding its way down by the river. Hassan was delighted with the progress Bahi had made, and ordered that three or four boys should at once be placed for instruction under each of the men who had learned trades at Penang.

There was much regret on both sides when the *Serpent* again started down the river; for it was known that she would not return, as in a few months she would be sent to a Chinese station, and from there would go direct to England. The composition of her crew was already somewhat changed. Lieutenant Ferguson had received his promotion for the fight with the prahus, and had been appointed to the command of a gunboat whose captain had been invalided home. Lieutenant Hopkins was now the *Serpent's* first lieutenant, and Morrison was second. Harry Parkhurst was third lieutenant, Dick Balderson, to the regret of both, having left the ship on his promotion, and having been transferred as third lieutenant to Captain Ferguson's craft. Both have since kept up a correspondence with Bahi, who has married a neighboring chief, and who tells them that the river is prospering greatly, and that, although he assumes no authority, her father is everywhere regarded as the paramount chief of the district. From time to time each receives chests filled with spices, silks, and other Malay products, and sends back in return European articles of utility to the rajah, for such is the rank that Hassan has now acquired on the river. ☾

chapter 3

The Pirate Who Could Not Swim

BY FRANK RICHARD STOCKTON

W hen the little fleet of Spanish vessels, including the one which had been captured by Bartholemy Portuguez and his men, were on their way to Campeachy, they met with very stormy weather so that they were separated, and the ship that contained Bartholemy and his companions arrived first at the port for which they were bound.

The captain, who had Bartholemy and the others in charge, did not know what an important capture he had made; he supposed that these pirates were ordinary buccaneers, and it appears that it was his intention to keep them as his own private prisoners, for, as they were all very able-bodied men, they would be extremely useful on a ship. But when his vessel was safely moored, and it became known in the town that he had a company of pirates on board, a great many people came from shore to see these savage men, who were probably looked upon very much as if they were a menagerie of wild beasts brought from foreign lands.

Among the sightseers who came to the ship was a merchant of the town who had seen Bartholemy before, and who had heard of his various exploits. He therefore went to the captain of the vessel and informed him that he had on board one of the very worst pirates in the whole world, whose wicked deeds were well known in various parts of the West Indies, and who ought immediately to be delivered up to the civil authorities. This proposal, however, met with no favor from the Spanish captain, who had found Bartholemy a very quiet man, and could see that he was a very strong one, and he did not at all desire to give up such a valuable addition to his crew. But the merchant grew very angry, for he knew that Bartholemy had inflicted great injury on Spanish commerce, and as the captain would not listen to him, he went to the Governor of the town and reported the case. When this dignitary heard the story he immediately sent a party of officers to the ship, and commanded the captain to deliver the pirate leader into their charge. The other men were left where they were, but Bartholemy was taken away and confined in another ship. The merchant, who seemed to know a great deal about him, informed the authorities that this terrible pirate had been captured several times, but that he had always managed to escape, and, therefore, he was put in irons, and preparations were made to execute him on the next day; for, from what he had heard, the Governor considered that this pirate was no better than a wild beast, and that he should be put to death without even the formality of a trial.

But there was a Spanish soldier on board the ship who seemed to have had some pity, or perhaps some admiration, for the daring pirate, and he thought that if he were to be hung the next day it was no more than right to let him know it, so that when he went in to take some food to Bartholemy he told him what was to happen.

Now this pirate captain was a man who always wanted to have a share in what was to happen, and he immediately racked his brain to find out what he could do in this case. He had never been in a more desperate situation, but he did not lose heart, and immediately set to work to free himself from his irons, which were probably very clumsy affairs. At last, caring little how much he scratched and tore his skin, he succeeded in getting rid of his fetters, and could move about as freely as a tiger in a cage. To get out of this cage was Bartholemy's first object. It would be comparatively easy, because in the course of time some one would come into the hold, and the athletic buccaneer thought that he could easily get the better of whoever might open the hatch. But the next act in this truly melodramatic performance would be a great deal more difficult; for in order to escape from the ship it would be absolutely necessary for Bartholemy to swim to shore, and he did not know how to swim, which seems a strange failing in a hardy sailor with so many other nautical accomplishments. In the rough hold where he was shut up, our pirate, peering about, anxious and earnest, discovered two large, earthen jars in which wine had been brought from Spain, and with these he determined to make a sort of life preserver. He found some pieces of oiled cloth, which he tied tightly over the open mouths of the jars and fastened them with cords. He was satisfied that this unwieldy contrivance would support him in the water.

Among other things he had found in his rummagings about the hold was an old knife, and with this in his hand he now sat waiting for a good opportunity to attack his sentinel.

This came soon after nightfall. A man descended with a lantern to see that the prisoner was still secure—let us hope that it was not the soldier who had kindly informed him of his fate—and as soon as he was fairly in the hold Bartholemy sprang upon him. There was a fierce struggle, but the pirate was quick and powerful, and the sentinel was soon dead. Then, carrying his two jars, Bartholemy climbed swiftly and noiselessly up the short ladder, came out on deck in the darkness, made a rush toward the side of the ship, and leaped overboard. For a moment he sank below the surface, but the two airtight jars quickly rose and bore him up with them. There was a bustle on board the ship, there was some random firing of muskets in the direction of the splashing that the watch had heard, but none of the balls struck the pirate or his jars, and he soon floated out of sight and hearing. Kicking out with his legs, and paddling as well as he could with one hand while he held on to the jars with the other, he at last managed to reach the land, and ran as fast as he could into the dark woods beyond the town.

Bartholemy was now greatly in fear that, when his escape was discovered, he would be tracked by bloodhounds—for these dogs were much used by the Spaniards in pursuing escaping slaves or prisoners—and he therefore did not feel safe in immediately making his way along the coast, which was what he wished to do. If the hounds should get upon his trail, he was a lost man. The desperate pirate, therefore, determined to give the bloodhounds no chance to follow him, and for three days he remained in a marshy forest, in the dark recesses of which he could hide, and where the water, which covered the ground, prevented the dogs from following his scent. He had nothing to eat except a few roots of water plants, but he was accustomed to privation, and these kept him alive. Often he heard the hounds baying on the dry land adjoining the marsh, and sometimes he saw at night distant torches, which he was sure were carried by men who were hunting for him.

But at last the pursuit seemed to be given up; and hearing no more dogs and seeing no more flickering lights, Bartholemy left the marsh and set out on his long journey down the coast. The place he wished to reach was called Golpho Triste, which was forty leagues away, but where he had reason to suppose he would find some friends. When he came out from among the trees, he mounted a small hill and looked back upon the town. The public square was lighted, and there in the middle of it he saw the gallows which had been erected for his execution, and this sight, doubtless, animated him very much during the first part of his journey.

The terrible trials and hardships which Bartholemy experienced during his tramp along the coast were such as could have been endured only by one of the strongest and toughest of men. He had found in the marsh an old gourd, or calabash, which he had filled with freshwater—for he could expect nothing but seawater during his journey—and as for solid food he had nothing but the raw shellfish that he found upon the rocks; but after a diet of roots, shellfish must have been a very agreeable change, and they gave him all the strength and vigor he needed. Very often he found streams and inlets that he was obliged to ford, and as he could see that they were always filled with alligators, the passage of them was not very pleasant. His method of getting across one of these narrow streams, was to hurl rocks into the water until he had frightened away the alligators immediately in front of him, and then, when he had made for himself what seemed to be a free passage, he would dash in and hurry across.

At other times great forests stretched down to the very coast, and through these he was obliged to make his way, although he could hear the roars and screams of wild beasts all about him. Anyone who is afraid to go down into a dark cellar to get some apples from a barrel at the foot of the stairs can have no idea of the sort of mind possessed by Bartholemy Portuguez. The animals might howl around him and glare at him with their shining eyes, and the alligators might lash the water into foam with their great tails, but he was bound for Golpho Triste and was not to be stopped on his way by anything alive.

But at last he came to something not alive, which seemed to be an obstacle that would certainly get the better of him. This was a wide river, flowing through the inland country into the sea. He made his way up the shore of this river for a considerable distance, but it grew but little narrower, and he could see no chance of getting across. He could not swim and he had no wine jars now with which to buoy himself up, and if he had been able to swim he would probably have been eaten up by alligators soon after he left the shore. But a man in his situation would not be likely to give up readily; he had done so much that he was ready to do more if he could only find out what to do.

Now a piece of good fortune happened to him, although to an ordinary traveler it might have been considered a matter of no importance whatever. On the edge of the shore, where it had floated down from some region higher up the river, Bartholemy perceived an old board, in which there were some long and heavy rusty nails. Greatly encouraged by this discovery the indefatigable traveler set about a work that resembled that of the old woman who wanted a needle, and who began to rub a crowbar on a stone in order to reduce it to the proper size. Bartholemy carefully knocked all the nails out of the board, and then finding a large flat stone, he rubbed down one of them until he had formed it into the shape of a rude knife blade, which he made as sharp as he could. Then with these tools he undertook the construction of a raft, working away like a beaver, and using the sharpened nails instead of his teeth. He cut down a number of small trees, and when he had enough of these slender trunks he bound them together with reeds and osiers, which he found on the river bank. So, after infinite labor and trial he constructed a raft that would bear him on the surface of the water. When he had launched this he got upon it, gathering up his legs so as to keep out of reach of the alligators, and with a long pole pushed himself off from shore. Sometimes paddling and sometimes pushing his pole against the bottom, he at last got across the river and took up his journey upon dry land.

But our pirate had not progressed very far upon the other side of the river before he met with a new difficulty of a very formidable character. This was a great forest of mangrove trees, which grow in muddy and watery places and which have many roots, some coming down from the branches, and some extending themselves in a hopeless tangle in the water and mud. It would have been impossible for even a stork to walk through this forest, but as there was no way of getting around it Bartholemy determined to go through it, even if he could not walk. No athlete of the present day, no matter if he should be a most accomplished circus-man, could reasonably expect to perform the feat which this bold pirate successfully accomplished. For five or six leagues he went through that mangrove forest, never once setting his foot upon the ground—by which is meant mud, water, and roots—but swinging himself by his hands and arms, from branch to branch, as if he had been a great ape, only resting occasionally, drawing himself upon a stout limb where he might sit for a while and get his breath. If he had slipped while he was swinging from one limb to another and had gone down into the mire and roots beneath him, it is likely that he would never have been able to get out alive. But he made no slips. He might not have had the agility and grace of a trapeze performer, but his grasp was powerful and his arms were strong, and so he swung and clutched, and clutched and swung, until he had gone entirely through the forest and had come out on the open coast.

It was full two weeks from the time that Bartholemy began his most adventurous and difficult journey before he reached the little town of Golpho Triste, where, as he had hoped, he found some of his buccaneer friends. Now that his hardships and dangers were over, and when, instead of roots and shellfish, he could sit down to good, plentiful meals, and stretch himself upon a comfortable bed, it might have been supposed that Bartholemy would have given himself a long rest, but this hardy pirate had no desire for a vacation at this time. Instead of being worn out and exhausted by his amazing exertions and semistarvation, he arrived among his friends vigorous and energetic and exceedingly anxious to recommence business as soon as possible. He told them of all that had happened to him, what wonderful good fortune had come to him, and what terrible bad fortune had quickly followed it, and when he had related his adventures and his dangers he astonished even his piratical friends by asking them to furnish him with a small vessel and about twenty men, in order that he might go back and revenge himself, not only for what had happened to him, but for what would have happened if he had not taken his affairs into his own hands.

To do daring and astounding deeds is part of the business of a pirate, and although it was an uncommonly bold enterprise that Bartholemy contemplated, he got his vessel and he got his men, and away he sailed. After a voyage of about eight days he came in sight of the little seaport town, and sailing slowly along the coast, he waited until nightfall before entering the harbor. Anchored at a considerable distance from shore was the great Spanish ship on which he had been a prisoner, and from which he would have been taken and hung in the public square; the

sight of the vessel filled his soul with a savage fury known only to pirates and bulldogs.

As the little vessel slowly approached the great ship, the people on board the latter thought it was a trading vessel from shore, and allowed it to come alongside, such small craft seldom coming from the sea. But the moment Bartholemy reached the ship he scrambled up its side almost as rapidly as he had jumped down from it with his two wine jars a few weeks before, and every one of his crew, leaving their own vessel to take care of itself, scrambled up after him.

Nobody on board was prepared to defend the ship. It was the same old story; resting quietly in a peaceful harbor, what danger had they to expect? As usual the pirates had everything their own way; they were ready to fight, and the others were not, and they were led by a man who was determined to take that ship without giving even a thought to the ordinary alternative of dying in the attempt. The affair was more of a massacre than a combat, and there were people on board who did not know what was taking place until the vessel had been captured.

As soon as Bartholemy was master of the great vessel he gave orders to slip the cable and hoist the sails, for he was anxious to get out of that harbor as quickly as possible. The fight had apparently attracted no attention in the town, but there were ships in the port whose company the bold buccaneer did not at all desire, and as soon as possible he got his grand prize under way and went sailing out of the port. Now, indeed, was Bartholemy triumphant; the ship he had captured was a finer one and a richer one than that other vessel which had been taken from him. It was loaded with valuable merchandise, and we may here remark that for some reason or other all Spanish vessels of that day that were so unfortunate as to be taken by pirates, seemed to be richly laden.

If our bold pirate had sung wild pirate songs, as he passed the flowing bowl while carousing with his crew in the cabin of the Spanish vessel he had first captured, he now sang wilder songs, and passed more flowing bowls, for this prize was a much greater one than the first. If Bartholemy could have communicated his great good fortune to the other buccaneers in the West Indies, there would have been a boom in piracy which would have threatened great danger to the honesty and integrity of the seafaring men of that region.

But nobody, not even a pirate, has any way of finding out what is going to happen next, and if Bartholemy had had an idea of the fluctuations that were about to occur in the market in which he had made his investments he would have been in a great hurry to sell all his stock very much below par. The fluctuations referred to occurred on the ocean, near the island of Pinos, and came in the shape of great storm waves, which blew the Spanish vessel with all its rich cargo, and its triumphant pirate crew, high up upon the cruel rocks, and wrecked it absolutely and utterly. Bartholemy and his men barely managed to get into a little boat, and row themselves away. All the wealth and treasure that had come to them with the capture of the Spanish vessel, all the power that the possession of that vessel gave them, and all the wild joy that came to them with riches and power, were lost to them in as short a space of time as it had taken to gain them.

In the way of well-defined and conspicuous ups and downs, few lives surpassed that of Bartholemy Portuguez. But after this he seems, in the language of the old English song, "All in the downs." He had many

adventures after the desperate affair in the Bay of Campeachy, but they must all have turned out badly for him, and, consequently, very well, it is probable, for divers and sundry Spanish vessels, and, for the rest of his life, he bore the reputation of an unfortunate pirate. He was one of those men whose success seemed to have depended entirely upon his own exertions. If there happened to be the least chance of his doing anything, he generally did it; Spanish cannon, well-armed Spanish crews, manacles, imprisonment, the dangers of the ocean to a man who could not swim, bloodhounds, alligators, wild beasts, awful forests impenetrable to common men, all these were bravely met and triumphed over by Bartholemy.

But when he came to ordinary good fortune, such as any pirate might expect, Bartholemy the Portuquez found that he had no chance at all. But he was not a common pirate, and was, therefore, obliged to be content with his uncommon career. He eventually settled in the island of Jamaica, but nobody knows what became of him. If it so happened that he found himself obliged to make his living by some simple industry, such as the selling of fruit upon a street corner, it is likely he never disposed of a banana or an orange unless he jumped at the throat of a passerby and compelled him to purchase. As for sitting still and waiting for customers to come to him, such a man as Bartholemy would not be likely to do anything so commonplace. ☾

chapter 4

The Life, Atrocities, and Bloody Death of Blackbeard

BY CHARLES ELLMS

Edward Teach was a native of Bristol, and having gone to Jamaica, frequently sailed from that port as one of the crew of a privateer during the French war. In that station he gave frequent proofs of his boldness and personal courage; but he was not entrusted with any command until Captain Benjamin Hornigold gave him the command of a prize that he had taken.

In the spring of 1717, Hornigold and Teach sailed from Providence for the continent of America, and on their way captured a small vessel with 120 barrels of flour, which they put on board their own vessel. They also seized two other vessels; from one they took some gallons of wine, and from the other, plunder to a considerable value. After cleaning upon the coast of Virginia, they made a prize of a large French Guineaman bound to Martinique, and Teach obtaining the command of her, went to the island of Providence, and surrendered to the king's clemency.

Teach now began to act an independent part. He mounted his vessel with forty guns, and named her the *Queen Anne's Revenge*. Cruising near the island of St. Vincent, he took a large ship, called the *Great Allan*, and after having plundered her of what he deemed proper, set her on fire. A few days after, Teach encountered the *Scarborough* man-of-war, and engaged her for some hours; but perceiving his strength and resolution, she retired, and left Teach to pursue his depredations. His next adventure was with a sloop of ten guns, commanded by Major Bonnet, and these two men cooperated for some time: but Teach finding him unacquainted with naval affairs, gave the command of Bonnet's ship to Richards, one of his own crew, and entertained Bonnet on board his own vessel. Watering at Turniff, they discovered a sail, and Richards with the *Revenge* slipped her cable, and ran out to meet her. Upon seeing the black flag hoisted, the vessel struck, and came-to under the stern of Teach the commodore. This was the *Adventure* from Jamaica. They took the captain and his men on board the great ship, and manned his sloop for their own service.

Weighing from Turniff, where they remained during a week, and sailing to the bay, they found there a ship and four sloops. Teach hoisted his flag, and began to fire at them, upon which the captain and his men left their ship and fled to the shore. Teach burned two of these sloops, and let the other three depart.

They afterwards sailed to different places, and having taken two small vessels, anchored off the bar of Charleston for a few days. Here they captured a ship bound for England, as she was coming out of the harbor. They next seized a vessel coming out of Charleston, and two pinks coming into the same harbor, together with a brigantine with fourteen Negroes. The audacity of these transactions, performed in sight of the town, struck the inhabitants with terror, as they had been lately visited by some other notorious pirates. Meanwhile, there were eight sail in the harbor, none of which durst set to sea for fear of falling into the hands of Teach. The trade of this place was totally interrupted, and the inhabitants were abandoned to despair. Their calamity was greatly augmented from this circumstance, that a long and desperate war with the natives had just terminated, when they began to be infested by these robbers.

Teach having detained all the persons taken in these ships as prisoners, they were soon in great want of medicines, and he had the audacity to demand a chest from the governor. This demand was made in a manner not less daring than insolent. Teach sent Richards, the captain of the *Revenge*, with Mr. Marks, one of the prisoners, and several others, to present their request. Richards informed the governor that unless their demand was granted, and he and his companions returned in safety, every prisoner on board the captured ships should instantly be slain, and the vessels consumed to ashes.

During the time that Mr. Marks was negotiating with the governor, Richards and his associates walked the streets at pleasure, while indignation flamed from every eye against them, as the robbers of their property, and the terror of their country. Though the affront thus offered to the Government was great and most audacious, yet, to preserve the lives of so many men, they granted their request, and sent on board a chest valued at three or four hundred pounds.

Teach, as soon as he received the medicines and his fellow pirates, pillaged the ships of gold and provisions, and then dismissed the prisoners with their vessels. From the bar of Charleston they sailed to North Carolina. Teach now began to reflect how he could best secure the spoil, along with some of the crew who were his favorites. Accordingly, under pretence of cleaning, he ran his vessel on shore, and grounded; then ordered the men in Hands' sloop to come to his assistance, which they endeavoring to do, also ran aground, and so they were both lost. Then Teach went into the tender with forty hands, and upon a sandy island, about a league from shore, where there was neither bird no beast, nor herb for their subsistence, he left seventeen of his crew, who must inevitably have perished had not Major Bonnet received intelligence of their miserable situation, and sent a long boat for them. After this barbarous deed Teach, with the remainder of his crew, went and surrendered to the governor of North Carolina, retaining all the property that had been acquired by his fleet.

The temporary suspension of the depredations of Blackbeard, for so he was now called, did not proceed from a conviction of his former errors, or a determination to reform, but to prepare for future and more extensive exploits. As governors are but men, and not unfrequently by no means possessed of the most virtuous principles, the gold of Blackbeard rendered him comely in the governor's eyes, and, by his influence, he obtained a legal right to the great ship called the *Queen Anne's Revenge*. By order of the governor, a court of vice-admiralty was held at Bathtown, and that vessel was condemned as a lawful prize that he had taken from the Spaniards, though it was a well-known fact that she belonged to English merchants. Before he entered upon his new adventures, he married a young woman of about sixteen years of age, the governor himself attending the ceremony. It was reported that this was only his fourteenth wife, about twelve of whom were yet alive; and though this woman was young and amiable, he behaved towards her in a manner so brutal, that it was shocking to all decency and propriety, even among his abandoned crew of pirates.

In his first voyage, Blackbeard directed his course to the Bermudas, and meeting with two or three English vessels, emptied them of their stores and other necessaries, and allowed them to proceed. He also met with two French vessels bound for Martinique, the one light, and the other laden with sugar and cocoa: he put the men on board the latter into the former, and allowed her to depart. He brought the freighted vessel into North Carolina, where the governor and Blackbeard shared the prizes. Nor did their audacity and villany stop here. Teach and some of his abandoned crew waited upon his excellency, and swore that they had seized the French ship at sea, without a soul on board; therefore a court was called, and she was condemned, the honorable governor received sixty hogsheads of sugar for his share, his secretary twenty, and the pirates the remainder. But as guilt always inspires suspicion, Teach was afraid that some one might arrive in the harbor who might detect the roguery: therefore, upon pretence that she was leaky, and might sink, and so stop up the entrance to the harbor where she lay, they obtained the governor's liberty to drag her into the river, where she was set on fire, and when burnt down to the water, her bottom was sunk, that so she might never rise in judgment against the governor and his confederates.

Blackbeard now being in the province of Friendship, passed several months in the river, giving and receiving visits from the planters; while he traded with the vessels that came to that river, sometimes in the way of lawful commerce, and sometimes in his own way. When he chose to appear the honest man, he made fair purchases on equal barter; but when this did not suit his necessities, or his humor, he would rob at pleasure, and leave them to seek their redress from the governor; and the better to cover his intrigues with his excellency, he would sometimes outbrave him to his face, and administer to him a share of that contempt and insolence that he so liberally bestowed upon the rest of the inhabitants of the province.

But there are limits to human insolence and depravity. The captains of the vessels who frequented that river, and had been so often harrassed and plundered by Blackbeard, secretly consulted with some of the planters what measures to pursue, in order to banish such an infamous miscreant from their coasts, and to bring him to deserved punishment. Convinced from long experience that the governor himself, to whom it belonged, would give no redress, they represented the matter to the governor of Virginia, and entreated that an armed force might be sent from the men-of-war lying there, either to take or to destroy those pirates who infested their coast.

Upon this representation, the governor of Virginia consulted with the captains of the two men-of-war as to the best measures to be adopted. It was resolved that the governor should hire two small vessels, which could pursue Blackbeard into all his inlets and creeks; that they should be manned from the men-of-war, and the command given to Lieutenant Maynard, an experienced and resolute officer. When all was ready for his departure, the governor called an assembly, in which it was resolved to issue a proclamation, offering a great reward to any who, within a year, should take or destroy any pirate.

Upon the 17th of November 1717, Maynard left James's river in quest of Blackbeard, and on the evening of the 21st came in sight of the pirate. This expedition was fitted out with all possible expedition and secrecy, no boat being permitted to pass that might convey any intelligence, while care was taken to discover where the pirates were lurking. His excellency the governor of Bermuda, and his secretary, however, having obtained information of the intended expedition, the latter wrote a letter to Blackbeard, intimating, that he had sent him four of his men, who were all he could meet within or about town, and so bade him be on his guard. These men were sent from Bathtown to the place where Blackbeard lay, about the distance of twenty leagues.

The hardened and infatuated pirate, having been often deceived by false intelligence, was the less attentive to this information, nor was he convinced of its accuracy until he saw the sloops sent to apprehend him. Though he had then only twenty men on board, he prepared to give battle. Lieutenant Maynard arrived with his sloops in the evening, and anchored, as he could not venture, under cloud of night, to go into the place where Blackbeard lay. The latter spent the night in drinking with the master of a trading vessel, with the same indifference as if no danger had been near. Nay, such was the desperate wickedness of this villain, that, it is reported, during the carousals of that night, one of his men asked him, "In case any thing should happen to him during the engagement with the two sloops that were waiting to attack him in the morning, whether his wife knew where he had buried his money?" when he impiously replied, "That nobody but himself and the devil knew where it was, and the longest liver should take all."

In the morning Maynard weighed, and sent his boat to sound, which coming near the pirate, received her fire. Maynard then hoisted royal colors, and made directly towards Blackbeard with every sail and oar. In a little time the pirate ran aground, and so also did the king's vessels. Maynard lightened his vessel of the ballast and water, and made towards Blackbeard. Upon this he hailed him in his own rude style, "D—n you for villains, who are you, and from whence come you?" The lieutenant answered, "You may see from our colors we are no pirates." Blackbeard bade him send his boat on board, that he might see who he was. But Maynard replied, "I cannot spare my boat, but I will come on board of you as soon as I can with my sloop." Upon this Blackbeard took a glass of liquor and drank to him, saying, "I'll give no quarter nor take any from you." Maynard replied, that he expected no quarter from him, nor should he give him any.

During this dialogue the pirate's ship floated, and the sloops were rowing with all expedition towards him. As she came near, the pirate fired a broadside, charged with all manner of small shot, which killed or wounded twenty men. Blackbeard's ship in a little after fell broad-side to the shore; one of the sloops called the *Ranger*, also fell astern. But Maynard finding that his own sloop had way, and would soon be on board of Teach, ordered all his men down, while himself and the man at the helm, who he commanded to lie concealed, were the only persons who remained on deck. He at the same time desired them to take their pistols, cutlasses, and swords, and be ready for action upon his call, and, for greater expedition, two ladders were placed in the hatchway. When the king's sloop boarded, the pirate's case boxes, filled with powder, small shot, slugs, and pieces of lead and iron, with a quick-match in the mouth of them, were thrown into Maynard's sloop. Fortunately, however, the men being in the hold, they did small injury on the present occasion, though they are usually very destructive. Blackbeard seeing few or no hands upon deck, cried to his men that they were all knocked on the head except three or four; "And therefore," said he, "let us jump on board, and cut to pieces those that are alive."

Upon this, during the smoke occasioned by one of these case boxes, Blackbeard, with fourteen of his men, entered, and were not perceived until the smoke was dispelled. The signal was given to Maynard's men, who rushed up in an instant. Blackbeard and the lieutenant exchange shots, and the pirate was wounded; they then engaged sword in hand, until the sword of the lieutenant broke, but fortunately one of his men at that instant gave Blackbeard a terrible wound in the neck and throat. The most desperate and bloody conflict ensued:—Maynard with twelve men, and Blackbeard with fourteen. The sea was dyed with blood all around the vessel, and uncommon bravery was displayed upon both sides. Though the pirate was wounded by the first shot from Maynard, though he had received twenty cuts, and as many shots, he fought with desperate valor; but at length, when in the act of cocking his pistol, fell down dead. By this time eight of his men had fallen, and the rest being wounded, cried out for quarter, which was granted, as the ringleader was slain. The other sloop also attacked the men who remained in the pirate vessels, until they also cried out for quarter. And such was the desperation of Blackbeard, that, having small hope of escaping, he had placed a Negro with a match at the gunpowder door, to blow up the ship the moment that he should have been boarded by the king's men, in order to involve the whole in general ruin. That destructive broadside at the commencement of the action, which at first appeared so unlucky, was, however, the means of their preservation from the intended destruction.

Maynard severed the pirate's head from his body, suspended it upon his bowsprit-end, and sailed to Bathtown, to obtain medical aid for his wounded men. In the pirate sloop several letters and papers were found, which Blackbeard would certainly have destroyed previous to the engagement, had he not determined to blow her up upon his being taken, that disclosed the whole villainy between the honorable governor of Bermuda and his honest secretary on the one hand, and the notorious pirate on the other, who had now suffered the just punishment of his crimes.

Scarcely was Maynard returned to Bathtown, when he boldly went and made free with the sixty hogsheads of sugar in the possession of the governor, and the twenty in that of his secretary.

After his men had been healed at Bathtown, the lieutenant proceeded to Virginia, with the head of Blackbeard still suspended on his bowsprit-end, as a trophy of his victory, to the great joy of all the inhabitants. The prisoners were tried, condemned, and executed; and thus all the crew of that infernal miscreant, Blackbeard, were destroyed, except two. One of these was taken out of a trading vessel, only the day before the engagement, in which he received no less than seventy wounds, of all which he was cured. The other was Israel Hands, who was master of the *Queen Anne's Revenge*; he was taken at Bathtown, being wounded in one of Blackbeard's savage humors. One night Blackbeard, drinking in his cabin with Hands, the pilot, and another man, without any pretence, took a small pair of pistols, and cocked them under the table; which being perceived by the man, he went on deck, leaving the captain, Hands, and the pilot together. When his pistols were prepared, he extinguished the candle, crossed his arms, and fired at his company. The one pistol did no execution, but the other wounded Hands in the knee. Interrogated concerning the meaning of this, he answered with an imprecation, "That if he did not now and then kill one of them, they would forget who he was." Hands was eventually tried and condemned, but as he was about to be executed, a vessel arrived with a proclamation prolonging the time of his Majesty's pardon, which Hands pleading, he was saved from a violent and shameful death.

In the commonwealth of pirates, he who goes the greatest length of wickedness, is looked upon with a kind of envy amongst them, as a person of a most extraordinary gallantry; he is therefore entitled to be distinguished by some post, and, if such a one has but courage, he must certainly be a great man. The hero of whom we are writing was thoroughly accomplished in this way, and some of his frolics of wickedness were as extravagant as if he aimed at making his men believe he was a devil incarnate. Being one day at sea, and a little flushed with drink, "Come," said he, "let us make a hell of our own, and try how long we can bear it." Accordingly he, with two or three others, went down into the hold, and closing up all the hatches, filled several pots full of brimstone, and other combustible matter; they then set it on fire, and so continued till they were almost suffocated, when some of the men cried out for air; at length he opened the hatches, not a little pleased that he had held out the longest.

Those of his crew who were taken alive, told a story that may appear a little incredible. That once, upon a cruise, they found out that they had a man on board more than their crew; such a one was seen several days amongst them, sometimes below, and sometimes upon deck, yet no man in the ship could give any account who he was, or from whence he came; but that he disappeared a little before they were cast away in their great ship, and, it seems, they verily believed it was the devil.

One would think these things should have induced them to reform their lives; but being so many reprobates together, they encouraged and spirited one another up in their wickedness, to which a continual course of drinking did not a little contribute. In Blackbeard's journal, which was taken, there were several memoranda of the following nature, all written with his own hand. "Such a day, rum all out—our company somewhat sober—a d—d confusion amongst us!—rogues a plotting—great talk of separation. So I looked sharp for a prize—such a day took one, with a great deal of liquor on board—so kept the company hot, d—d hot, then all things went well again."

We shall close the narrative of this extraordinary man's life by an account of the cause why he was denominated Blackbeard. He derived this name from his long Blackbeard, which, like a frightful meteor, covered his whole face, and terrified all America more than any comet that had ever appeared. He was accustomed to twist it with ribbon in small quantities, and turn them about his ears. In time of action he wore a sling over his shoulders with three brace of pistols. He stuck lighted matches under his hat, which appeared on both sides of his face and eyes, naturally fierce and wild, made him such a figure that the human imagination cannot form a conception of a fury more terrible and alarming; and if he had the appearance and look of a fury, his actions corresponded with that character. ☾

chapter 5

The Real Captain Kidd
BY FRANK RICHARD STOCKTON

Willliam Kidd, or Robert Kidd, as he is sometimes called, was a sailor in the merchant service who had a wife and family in New York. He was a very respectable man and had a good reputation as a seaman, and about 1690, when there was war between England and France, Kidd was given the command of a privateer, and having had two or three engagements with French vessels he showed himself to be a brave fighter and a prudent commander.

Some years later he sailed to England, and, while there, he received an appointment of a peculiar character. It was at the time when the King of England was doing his best to put down the pirates of the American coast, and Sir George Bellomont, the recently appointed Governor of New York, recommended Captain Kidd as a very suitable man to command a ship to be sent out to suppress piracy. When Kidd agreed to take the position of chief of marine police, he was not employed by the Crown, but by a small company of gentlemen of capital, who formed themselves into a sort of trust company, or society for the prevention of cruelty to merchantmen, and the object of their association was not

65

only to put down pirates, but to put some money in their own pockets as well.

Kidd was furnished with two commissions, one appointing him a privateer with authority to capture French vessels, and the other empowering him to seize and destroy all pirate ships. Kidd was ordered in his mission to keep a strict account of all booty captured, in order that it might be fairly divided among those who were stockholders in the enterprise, one-tenth of the total proceeds being reserved for the King.

Kidd sailed from England in the *Adventure*, a large ship with thirty guns and eighty men, and on his way to America he captured a French ship, which he carried to New York. Here he arranged to make his crew a great deal larger than had been thought necessary in England, and, by offering a fair share of the property he might confiscate on piratical or French ships, he induced a great many able seamen to enter his service, and when the *Adventure* left New York she carried a crew of one hundred and fifty-five men.

With a fine ship and a strong crew, Kidd now sailed out of the harbor with the ostensible purpose of putting down piracy in American waters, but the methods of this legally appointed marine policeman were very peculiar, and, instead of cruising up and down our coast, he gaily sailed away to the island of Madeira, and then around the Cape of Good Hope to Madagascar and the Red Sea, thus getting himself as far out of his regular beat as any New York constable would have been had he undertaken to patrol the dominions of the Khan of Tartary.

By the time Captain Kidd reached that part of the world he had been at sea for nearly a year without putting down any pirates or capturing any French ships. In fact, he had made no money whatever for himself or the stockholders of the company that had sent him out. His men, of course, must have been very much surprised at this unusual neglect of his own and his employers' interests, but when he reached the Red Sea, he boldly informed them that he had made a change in his business, and had decided that he would be no longer a suppressor of piracy, but would become a pirate himself; and, instead of taking prizes of French ships only—which he was legally empowered to do—he would try to capture any valuable ship he could find on the seas, no matter to what nation it belonged. He then went on to state that his present purpose in coming into those oriental waters was to capture the rich fleet from

Mocha that was due in the lower part of the Red Sea about that time.

The crew of the *Adventure*, who must have been tired of having very little to do and making no money, expressed their entire approbation of their captain's change of purpose, and readily agreed to become pirates.

Kidd waited a good while for the Mocha fleet, but it did not arrive, and then he made his first venture in actual piracy. He overhauled a Moorish vessel that was commanded by an English captain, and as England was not at war with Morocco, and as the nationality of the ship's commander should have protected him, Kidd thus boldly broke the marine laws that governed the civilized world and stamped himself an out-and-out pirate. After the exercise of considerable cruelty he extorted from his first prize a small amount of money; and although he and his men did not gain very much booty, they had whetted their appetites for more, and Kidd cruised savagely over the eastern seas in search of other spoils.

After a time the *Adventure* fell in with a fine English ship, called the *Royal Captain*, and although she was probably laden with a rich cargo, Kidd did not attack her. His piratical character was not yet sufficiently formed to give him the disloyal audacity that would enable him with his English ship and his English crew, to fall upon another English ship manned by another English crew. In time his heart might be hardened, but he felt that he could not begin with this sort of thing just yet. So the

Adventure saluted the *Royal Captain* with ceremonious politeness, and each vessel passed quietly on its way. But this conscientious consideration did not suit Kidd's crew. They had already had a taste of booty, and they were hungry for more, and when the fine English vessel, of which they might so easily have made a prize, was allowed to escape them, they were loud in their complaints and grumblings.

One of the men, a gunner, named William Moore, became actually impertinent upon the subject, and he and Captain Kidd had a violent quarrel, in the course of which the captain picked up a heavy iron-bound bucket and struck the dissatisfied gunner on the head with it. The blow was such a powerful one that the man's skull was broken, and he died the next day.

Captain Kidd's conscience seems to have been a good deal in his way; for although he had been sailing about in various eastern waters, taking prizes wherever he could, he was anxious that reports of his misdeeds should not get home before him. Having captured a fine vessel bound westward, he took from her all the booty he could, and then proceeded to arrange matters so that the capture of this ship should appear to be a legal transaction. The ship was manned by Moors and commanded by a Dutchman, and of course Kidd had no right to touch it, but the sharp-witted and businesslike pirate selected one of the passengers and made him sign a paper declaring that he was a Frenchman, and that he commanded the ship. When this statement had been sworn to before witnesses, Kidd put the document in his pocket so that if he were called upon to explain the transaction he might be able to show that he had good reason to suppose that he had captured a French ship, which, of course, was all right and proper.

Kidd now ravaged the East India waters with great success and profit, and at last he fell in with a very fine ship from Armenia, called the *Quedagh Merchant*, commanded by an Englishman. Kidd's conscience had been growing harder and harder every day, and he did not now hesitate to attack any vessel. The great merchantman was captured, and proved to be one of the most valuable prizes ever taken by a pirate, for Kidd's own share of the spoils amounted to more than sixth thousand dollars. This was such a grand haul that Kidd lost no time in taking his prize to some place where he might safely dispose of her cargo, and get rid of her passengers. Accordingly he sailed for Madagascar. While he was there he fell in with the first pirate vessel he had met since he had started out to put down piracy. This was a ship commanded by an English pirate named Culliford, and here would have been a chance for Captain Kidd to show that, although he might transgress the law himself, he would be true to his engagement not to allow other people to do so; but he had given up putting down piracy, and instead of apprehending Culliford he went into partnership with him, and the two agreed to go pirating together.

This partnership, however, did not continue long, for Captain Kidd began to believe that it was time for him to return to his native country and make a report of his proceedings to his employers. Having confined his piratical proceedings to distant parts of the world, he hoped that he would be able to make Sir George Bellomont and the other stockholders suppose that his booty was all legitimately taken from French vessels cruising in the east, and when the proper division should be made he would be able to quietly enjoy his portion of the treasure he had gained.

He did not go back in the *Adventure*, which was probably not large enough to carry all the booty he had amassed, but putting everything on board his latest prize, the *Quedagh Merchant*, he burned his old ship and sailed homeward.

When he reached the West Indies, however, our wary sea-robber was very much surprised to find that accounts of his evil deeds had reached America, and that the colonial authorities had been so much incensed by the news that the man who had been sent out to suppress piracy had become himself a pirate that they had circulated notices throughout the different colonies urging the arrest of Kidd if he should come into any American port. This was disheartening intelligence for the treasure-laden Captain Kidd, but he did not despair; he knew that the love of money was often as strong in the minds of human beings as the love of justice. Sir George Bellomont, who was now in New York, was one of the principal stockholders in the enterprise, and Kidd hoped that the rich share of the results of his industry that would come to the Governor might cause unpleasant reports to be disregarded. In this case he might yet return to his wife and family with a neat little fortune, and without danger of being called upon to explain his exceptional performances in the eastern seas.

Of course Kidd was not so foolish and rash as to sail into New York harbor on board the *Quedagh Merchant,* so he bought a small sloop and put the most valuable portion of his goods on board her, leaving his larger vessel, which also contained a great quantity of merchandise, in the charge of one of his confederates, and in the little sloop he cautiously approached the coast of New Jersey. His great desire was to find out what sort of a reception he might expect, so he entered Delaware Bay, and when he stopped at a little seaport in order to take in some supplies, he discovered that there was but small chance of his visiting his home and his family, and of making a report to his superior in the character of a deserving mariner who had returned after a successful voyage. Some people in the village recognized him, and the report soon spread to New York that the pirate Kidd was lurking about the coast. A sloop of war was sent out to capture his vessel, and finding that it was impossible to remain in the vicinity where he had been discovered, Kidd sailed northward and entered Long Island Sound.

Here the shrewd and anxious pirate began to act the part of the watch dog who has been killing sheep. In every way he endeavored to assume the appearance of innocence and to conceal every sign of misbehavior. He wrote to Sir George Bellomont that he should have called upon him in order to report his proceedings and hand over his profits, were it not for the wicked and malicious reports that had been circulated about him.

It was during this period of suspense, when the returned pirate did not know what was likely to happen, that it is supposed, by the believers in the hidden treasures of Kidd, that he buried his coin and bullion and his jewels, some in one place and some in another, so that if he were captured his riches would not be taken with him. Among the wild stories that were believed at that time, and for long years after, was one to the effect that Captain Kidd's ship was chased up the Hudson River by a man-of-war, and that the pirates, finding they could not get away, sank their ship and fled to the shore with all the gold and silver they could carry, which they afterwards buried at the foot of Dunderbergh Mountain. A great deal of rocky soil has been

turned over at different times in search of these treasures, but no discoveries of hidden coin have yet been reported. The fact is, however, that during this time of anxious waiting Kidd never sailed west of Oyster Bay in Long Island. He was afraid to approach New York, although he had frequent communication with that city, and was joined by his wife and family.

About this time occurred an incident that has given rise to all the stories regarding the buried treasure of Captain Kidd. The disturbed and anxious pirate concluded that it was a dangerous thing to keep so much valuable treasure on board his vessel, which might at any time be overhauled by the authorities, and he therefore landed at Gardiner's Island on the Long Island coast, and obtained permission from the proprietor to bury some of his superfluous stores upon his estate. This was a straightforward transaction. Mr. Gardiner knew all about the burial of the treasure, and when it was afterwards proved that Kidd was really a pirate, the hidden booty was all given up to the government.

This appears to be the only case in which it was positively known that Kidd buried treasure on our coast, and it has given rise to all the stories of the kind that have ever been told.

For some weeks Kidd's sloop remained in Long Island Sound, and then he took courage and went to Boston to see some influential people there. He was allowed to go freely about the city for a week, and then he was arrested.

The rest of Kidd's story is soon told; he was sent to England for trial, and there he was condemned to death, not only for the piracies he had committed, but also for the murder of William Moore. He was executed, and his body was hung in chains on the banks of the Thames, where for years it dangled in the wind, a warning to all evil-minded sailors.

About the time of Kidd's trial and execution a ballad was written that had a wide circulation in England and America. It was set to music, and for many years helped to spread the fame of this pirate. The ballad was a very long one, containing nearly twenty-six verses, and some of them run as follows:

> *My name was Robert Kidd, when I sailed, when I sailed,*
> *My name was Robert Kidd, when I sailed,*
> *My name was Robert Kidd,*
> *God's laws I did forbid,*
> *And so wickedly I did, when I sailed.*

My parents taught me well, when I sailed, when I sailed,
My parents taught me well when I sailed,
My parents taught me well
To shun the gates of hell,
But 'gainst them I rebelled, when I sailed.

I'd a Bible in my hand, when I sailed, when I sailed,
I'd a Bible in my hand when I sailed,
I'd a Bible in my hand,
By my father's great command,
And sunk it in the sand, when I sailed.

I murdered William Moore, as I sailed, as I sailed,
I murdered William Moore as I sailed,
I murdered William Moore,
And laid him in his gore,
Not many leagues from shore, as I sailed.

I was sick and nigh to death, when I sailed, when I sailed,
I was sick and nigh to death when I sailed,
I was sick and nigh to death,
And I vowed at every breath,
To walk in wisdom's ways, as I sailed.

I thought I was undone, as I sailed, as I sailed,
I thought I was undone, as I sailed,
I thought I was undone,
And my wicked glass had run,
But health did soon return, as I sailed.

My repentance lasted not, as I sailed, as I sailed,
My repentance lasted not, as I sailed,
My repentance lasted not,
My vows I soon forgot,
Damnation was my lot, as I sailed.

I spyed the ships from France, as I sailed, as I sailed,
I spyed the ships from France, as I sailed,
I spyed the ships from France,
To them I did advance,
And took them all by chance, as I sailed.

I spyed the ships of Spain, as I sailed, as I sailed,
I spyed the ships of Spain, as I sailed,
I spyed the ships of Spain,
I fired on them amain,
'Till most of them was slain, as I sailed.

I'd ninety bars of gold, as I sailed, as I sailed,
I'd ninety bars of gold, as I sailed,
I'd ninety bars of gold,
And dollars manifold,
With riches uncontrolled, as I sailed.

Thus being o'er-taken at last, I must die, I must die,
Thus being o'er-taken at last, I must die,
Thus being o'er-taken at last,
And into prison cast,
And sentence being passed, I must die.

Farewell, the raging main, I must die, I must die,
Farewell, the raging main, I must die,
Farewell, the raging main,
To Turkey, France, and Spain,
I shall ne'er see you again, I must die.

To Execution Dock I must go, I must go,
To Execution Dock I must go,
To Execution Dock,
Will many thousands flock,
But I must bear the shock, and must die.

Come all ye young and old, see me die, see me die,
Come all ye young and old, see me die,
Come all ye young and old,
You're welcome to my gold,
For by it I've lost my soul, and must die.

Take warning now by me, for I must die, for I must die,
Take warning now by me, for I must die,
Take warning now by me,
And shun bad company,
Lest you come to hell with me, for I die.

It is said that Kidd showed no repentance when he was tried, but insisted that he was the victim of malicious persons who swore falsely against him. And yet a more thoroughly dishonest rascal never sailed under the black flag. In the guise of an accredited officer of the government, he committed the crimes he was sent out to suppress; he deceived his men; he robbed and misused his fellow countrymen and his friends; and he even descended to the meanness of cheating and despoiling the natives of the West India Islands, with whom he traded. These people were in the habit of supplying pirates with food and other necessaries, and they always found their rough customers entirely honest, and willing to pay for what they received; for as the pirates made a practice of stopping at certain points for supplies, they wished, of course, to be on good terms with those who furnished them. But Kidd had no ideas of honor toward people of high or low degree. He would trade with the natives as if he intended to treat them fairly and pay for all he got; but when the time came for him to depart, and he was ready to weigh anchor, he would seize upon all the commodities he could lay his hands upon, and without paying a copper to the distressed and indignant Indians, he would gaily sail away, his black flag flaunting derisively in the wind.

But although in reality Captain Kidd was no hero, he has been known for a century and more as the great American pirate, and his name has been representative of piracy ever since. Years after he had been hung, when people heard that a vessel with a black flag, or one which looked black in the distance, flying from its rigging had been seen, they forgot that the famous pirate was dead, and imagined that Captain Kidd was visiting their part of the coast in order that he might find a good place to bury some treasure that it was no longer safe for him to carry about.

There were two great reasons for the fame of Captain Kidd. One of these was the fact that he had been sent out by important officers of the crown who expected to share the profits of his legitimate operations, but who were supposed by their enemies to be perfectly willing to take any sort of profits provided it could not be proved that they were the results of piracy, and who afterwards allowed Kidd to suffer for their sins as well as his own. These opinions introduced certain political features into his career and made him a very much talked of man. The greater reason for his fame, however, was the widespread belief in his buried treasures, and this made him the object of the most intense interest to hundreds of mis-guided people who hoped to be lucky enough to share his spoils.

There were other pirates on the American coast during the eighteenth century, and some of them became very well known, but their stories are not uncommon, and we need not tell them here. As our country became better settled, and as well-armed revenue cutters began to cruise up and down our Atlantic coast for the protection of our commerce, pirates be-came fewer and fewer, and even those who were still bold enough to ply their trade grew milder in their manners, less daring in their exploits, and—more important than anything else—so unsuccessful in their illegal enterprises that they were forced to admit that it was now more prof-itable to command or work a merchantman than endeavor to capture one, and so the sea-robbers of our coasts gradually passed away. ☾

chapter 6

The Life of Benito de Soto, the Pirate of the *Morning Star*

BY CHARLES ELLMS

The following narrative of the career of a desperate pirate who was executed in Gibraltar in the month of January 1830, is one of two letters from the pen of the author of the *Military Sketch-Book*. The writer says Benito de Soto "had been a prisoner in the garrison for nineteen months, during which time the British Government spared neither the pains nor expense to establish a full train of evidence against him. The affair had caused the greatest excitement here, as well as at Cadiz, owing to the development of the atrocities which marked the character of this man, and the diabolical gang of which he was the leader. Nothing else is talked of; and a thousand horrors are added to his guilt, which, although he was guilty enough, he has no right to bear. The following is all the authentic information I could collect concerning him. I have drawn it from his trial, from the confession of his accomplices, from the keeper of his prison, and not a little from his own lips. It will be found more interesting than all the tales and sketches furnished in the 'Annuals,' magazines, and other vehicles of invention, from the simple fact— that it is truth and not fiction."

Benito de Soto was a native of a small village near Courna; he was bred a mariner, and was in the guiltless exercise of his calling at Buenos Aires, in the year 1827. A vessel was there being fitted out for a voyage to the coast of Africa, for the smuggling of slaves; and as she required a strong crew, a great number of sailors were engaged, amongst whom was Soto. The Portuguese of South America have yet a privilege of dealing in slaves on a certain part of the African coast, but it was the intention of the captain of this vessel to exceed the limits of his trade, and to run farther down, so as to take his cargo of human beings from a part of the country that was proscribed, in the certainty of being there enabled to purchase slaves at a much lower rate than he could in the regular way; or, perhaps, to take away by force as many as he could stow away into his ship. He therefore required a considerable number of hands for the enterprise; and in such a traffic, it may be easily conceived, that the morals of the crew could not be a subject of much consideration with the employer. French, Spanish, Portuguese, and others were entered on board, most of them renegades, and they set sail on their evil voyage, with every hope of infamous success.

Those who deal in evil carry along with them the springs of their own destruction, upon which they will tread, in spite of every caution, and their imagined security is but the brink of the pit into which they are to fall. It was so with the captain of this slave ship. He arrived in Africa, took in a considerable number of slaves, and in order to complete his cargo, went on shore, leaving his mate in charge of the vessel. This mate was a bold, wicked, reckless and ungovernable spirit, and perceiving in Benito de Soto a mind congenial with his own, he fixed on him as a fit person to join in a design he had conceived, of running away with the vessel, and becoming a pirate. Accordingly the mate proposed his plan to Soto, who not only agreed to join in it, but declared that he himself had been contemplating a similar enterprise during the voyage. They both were at once of a mind, and they lost no time in maturing their plot.

Their first step was to break the matter to the other members of the crew. In this they proceeded cautiously, and succeeded so far as to gain over twenty-two of the whole, leaving eighteen who remained faithful to their trust. Every means were used to corrupt the well disposed; both persuasion and threats were resorted to, but without effect, and the leader of the conspiracy, the mate, began to despair of obtaining the desired object. Soto, however, was not so easily depressed. He at once decided on seizing the ship upon the strength of his party: and without consulting the mate, he collected all the arms of the vessel, called the conspirators together, put into each of their possession a cutlass and a brace of pistols, and arming himself in like manner, advanced at the head of the gang, drew his sword, and declared the mate to be the commander of the ship, and the men who joined him part owners. Still, those who had rejected the evil offer remained unmoved; on which Soto ordered out the boats, and pointing to the land, cried out, "There is the African coast; this is our ship—one or the other must be chosen by every man on board within five minutes."

This declaration, although it had the effect of preventing any resistance that might have been offered by the well disposed to the taking of the vessel, did not change them from their purpose; they still refused to join in the robbery, and entered one by one into the boat, at the orders of Soto, and with but one pair of oars (all that was allowed to them) put off for the shore, from which they were then ten miles distant. Had the weather continued calm, as it was when the boat left the ship, she would have made the shore by dusk; but unhappily a strong gale of wind set in shortly after her departure, and she was seen by Soto and his gang struggling with the billows and approaching night, at such a distance from the land as she could not possibly accomplish while the gale lasted. All on board the ship agreed in opinion that the boat could not live, as they flew away from her at the rate of ten knots an hour, under close reefed topsails, leaving their unhappy messmates to their inevitable fate. Those of the pirates who were lately executed at Cadiz declared that every soul in the boat perished.

The drunken uproar that that night reigned in the pirate ship was in horrid unison with the raging elements around her; contention and quarreling followed the brutal inebriety of the pirates; each evil spirit sought the mastery of the others, and Soto's, which was the fiend of all, began to grasp and grapple for its proper place—the head of such a diabolical community.

The mate (now the chief) at once gave the reins to his ruffian tyranny; and the keen eye of Soto saw that he who had fawned with him the day before, would next day rule him with an iron rod. Prompt in his actions as he was penetrating in his judgment, he had no sooner conceived a jealousy of the leader than he determined to put him aside; and as his rival lay in his drunken sleep, Soto put a pistol to his head, and deliberately shot him. For this act he excused himself to the crew, by stating to them that it was in their protection he did the act; that their interest was the other's death; and concluded by declaring himself their leader, and promising a golden harvest to their future labors, provided they obeyed him. Soto succeeded to the height of his wishes, and was unanimously hailed by the crew as their captain.

On board the vessel, as I before stated, were a number of slaves, and these the pirates had well secured under hatches. They now turned their attention to those half-starved, half-suffocated creatures—some were for throwing them overboard, while others, not less cruel, but more desirous of gain, proposed to take them to some port in one of those countries that deal in human beings, and there sell them. The latter recommendation was adopted, and Soto steered for the West Indies, where he received a good price for his slaves. One of those wretched creatures, a boy, he reserved as a servant for himself; and this boy was destined by Providence to be the witness of the punishment of those white men who tore away from their homes himself and his brethren. He alone will carry back to his country the truth of Heaven's retribution, and heal the wounded feelings of broken kindred with the recital of it.

The pirates now entered freely into their villainous pursuit, and plundered many vessels; amongst others was an American brig, the treatment of which forms the chef d'oeuvre of their atrocity. Having taken out of this brig all the valuables they could find, they hatched down all hands to the hold, except a black man, who was allowed to remain on deck for the special purpose of affording in his torture an amusing exhibition to Soto and his gang. They set fire to the brig, then lay to, to observe the progress of the flames; and as the miserable African bounded from rope to rope, now climbing to the masthead—now clinging to the shrouds—now leaping to one part of the vessel, and now to another—their enjoyment seemed raised to its heighest pitch. At length the hatches opened to the devouring element, the tortured victim of their fiendish cruelty fell exhausted into the flames, and the horrid and revolting scene closed amidst the shouts of the miscreants who had caused it.

Of their other exploits, that which ranks next in turpitude, and which led to their overthrow, was the piracy of the *Morning Star*. They fell in with that vessel near the island Ascension, in the year 1828, as she was on her voyage from Ceylon to England. This vessel, besides a valuable cargo, had on board several passengers, consisting of a major and his wife, an assistant surgeon, two civilians, about five and twenty invalid soldiers, and three or four of their wives. As soon as Benito de Soto perceived the ship, which was at daylight on the 21st of February, he called up all hands, and prepared for attacking her; he was at the time steering on an opposite course to that of the *Morning Star*. On reconnoitering her, he at first supposed she was a French vessel; but Barbazan, one of his crew, who was himself a Frenchman, assured him the ship was British. "So much the better," exclaimed Soto, in English (for he could speak that language), "we shall find the more booty." He then ordered the sails to be squared, and ran before the wind in chase of his plunder, from which he was about two leagues distant.

The *Defensor de Pedro*, the name of the pirate ship, was a fast sailer, but owing to the press of canvas which the *Morning Star* hoisted soon after the pirate had commenced the chase, he did not come up with her so quickly as he had expected: the delay caused great uneasiness to Soto, which he manifested by muttering curses, and restlessness of manner. Sounds of savage satisfaction were to be heard from every mouth but his at the prospect; he alone expressed his anticipated pleasure by oaths, menaces, and mental inquietude. While Barbazan was employed in super-intending the clearing of the decks, the arming and breakfasting of the men, he walked rapidly up and down, revolving in his mind the plan of the approaching attack, and when interrupted by any of the crew, he would run into a volley of imprecations. In one instance, he struck his black boy a violent blow with a telescope, because he asked him if he would have his morning cup of chocolate; as soon, however, as he set his studding sails, and perceived that he was gaining on the *Morning Star*, he became somewhat tranquil, began to eat heartily of cold beef, drank his chocolate at a draught, and coolly sat down on the deck to smoke a cigar.

In less than a quarter of an hour, the pirate had gained consider-able on the other vessel. Soto now, without rising from where he sat, ordered a gun, with blank cartridge, to be fired, and the British colors to be hoisted, but finding this measure had not the effect of bringing the *Morning Star* to, he cried out, "Shot the long gun and give it her point blank." The order was obeyed, but the shot fell short of the intention, on which he jumped up and cursed the fellows for bunglers who had fired the gun. He then ordered them to load with canister shot, and took the match in his own hand. He did not, however, fire immediately, but waited until he was nearly abreast of his victim; then directing the aim himself, and ordering a man to stand by the flag to haul it down, fired with an air that showed he was sure of his mark. He then ran to haul up the Colombian colors, and having done so, cried out through the speaking trumpet, "Lower your boat down this moment, and let your captain come on board with his papers."

During this fearful chase the people on board the *Morning Star* were in the greatest alarm; but however their apprehensions might have been excited, that courage, which is so characteristic of a British sailor, never for a moment forsook the captain. He boldly carried on sail, and although one of the men fell from a wound, and the ravages of the shot were every where around him, he determined not to strike. But unhappily he had not a single gun on board, and no small arms that could render his courage availing. The tears of the women, and the prudent advice of the passengers overcoming his resolution, he permitted himself to be guided by the general opinion. One of the passengers volunteered himself to go on board the pirate, and a boat was lowered for the purpose. Both vessels now lay to within fifty yards of each other, and a strong hope arose in those on board the *Morning Star*, that the gentleman who had volunteered to go to the pirate, might, through his exertions, avert, at least, the worst of the dreaded calamity.

Some people here, in their quiet security, have made no scruple of declaring, that the commanding officer of the soldiers on board should not have so tamely yielded to the pirate, particularly as he had his wife along with him, and consequently a misfortune to dread, that might be thought even worse than death, but all who knew the true state of the circumstances, and reflect upon it, will allow that he adopted the only chance of escaping that, which was to be most feared by a husband. The long gun, which was on a pivot in the center of the pirate ship, could in a few shots sink the *Morning Star*, and even had resistance been made to the pirates as they boarded her—had they been killed or made prisoners—the result would not be much better. It was evident that the *Defensor de Pedro* was the best sailer, consequently the *Morning Star* could not hope to escape; in fact, submission or total destruction was the only choice. The commanding officer, therefore, acted for the best when he recommended the former. There was some slight hope of escaping with life, and without personal abuse, by surrendering, but to contend must be inevitable death.

The gentleman who had gone in a boat to the pirate returned in a short time, exhibiting every proof of the ill treatment he had received from Soto and his crew. It appears that when the villains learned that he was not the captain, they fell upon and beat him, as well as the sailors along with him, in a most brutal manner, and with the most horrid imprecations told him, that if the captain did not instantly come, on his return to the vessel, they would blow the ship out of the water. This report as once decided the captain in the way he was to act. Without hesitation he stepped into the boat, taking with him his second mate, three soldiers, and a sailor boy, and proceeded to the pirate. On going on board that vessel, along with the mate, Soto, who stood near the mainmast, with his drawn cutlass in his hand, desired him to approach, while the mate was ordered, by Barbazan, to go to the forecastle. Both these unfortunate individuals obeyed, and were instantly slaughtered.

Soto now ordered six picked men to descend into the boat, amongst whom was Barbazan. To him the leader addressed his orders, the last of which was to take care to put all in the prize to death, and then sink her.

The six pirates, who proceeded to execute his savage demand, were all armed alike—they each carried a brace of pistols, a cutlass and a long knife. Their dress was composed of a sort of coarse cotton chequered jacket and trowsers, shirts that were open at the collar, red woollen caps, and broad canvas waistbelts, in which were the pistols and the knives. They were all athletic men, and seemed such as might well be trusted with the sanguinary errand on which they were despatched. While the boat was conveying them, Soto held in his hand a cutlass, reddened with the blood of the murdered captain, and stood scowling on them with silence, while another ruffian, with a lighted match, stood by the long gun, ready to support the boarding, if necessary, with a shot that would sweep the deck.

As the boarders approached the *Morning Star*, the terror of the females became excessive; they clung to their husbands in despair, who endeavored to allay their fears by their own vain hopes, assuring them that a quiet submission nothing more than the plunder of the vessel was to be apprehended. But a few minutes miserably undeceived them. The pirates rapidly mounted the side, and as they jumped on deck, commenced to cut right and left at all within their reach, uttering at the same time the most dreadful oaths. The females, screaming, hurried to hide themselves below as well as they were able, and the men fell or fled before the pirates, leaving them entire masters of the decks.

When the pirates had succeeded in effectually prostrating all the people on deck, they drove most of them below, and reserved the remainder to assist in their operations. Unless the circumstances be closely examined, it may be wondered how six men could have so easily overcome a crew of English seamen supported by about twenty soldiers with a major at their head—but it will not appear so surprising, when it is considered that the sailors were altogether unarmed, the soldiers were worn out invalids, and more particularly, that the pirate carried a heavy long gun, ready to sink her victim at a shot. Major Logie was fully impressed with the folly of opposing so powerful and desperate an enemy, and therefore advised submission as the only course for the safety of those under his charge, presuming no doubt that something like humanity might be found in the breasts even of the worst of men. But alas! he was woefully deceived in his estimate of the villains nature, and felt, when too late, that even death would have been preferable to the barbarous treatment he was forced to endure.

Beaten, bleeding, terrified, the men lay huddled together in the hold, while the pirates proceeded in their work of pillage and brutality. Every trunk was hauled forth, every portable article of value heaped for the plunder; money, plate, charts, nautical instruments, and seven parcels of valuable jewels, which formed part of the cargo; these were carried from below on the backs of those men whom the pirates selected to assist them, and for two hours they were thus employed, during which time Soto stood upon his own deck directing the operations; for the vessels were within a hundred yards of each other. The scene that took place in the cabin exhibited a licentious brutality. The sick officer, Mr. Gibson, was dragged from his berth, the clothes of the other passengers stripped from their backs, and the whole of the cabin passengers driven on deck, except the females, whom they locked up in the roundhouse on deck, and the steward, who was detained to serve the pirates with wine and eatables. This treatment, no doubt hastened the death of Gibson; the unfortunate gentleman did not long survive it. As the passengers were forced up the cabin ladder, the feelings of Major Logie, it may be imagined, were of the most heartrending description. In vain did he entreat to be allowed to remain; he was hurried away from even the chance of protecting his defenseless wife, and battened down with the rest in the hold, there to be racked with the fearful apprehensions of their almost certain doom.

The labors of the robbers being now concluded, they sat down to regale themselves, preparatory to the chef d'oeuvre of their diabolical enterprise; and a more terrible group of demidevils, the steward declares, could not be well imagined than commanded his attention at the cabin table. However, as he was a Frenchman, and naturally polite, he acquitted himself of the office of cup bearer, if not as gracefully, at least as anxiously, as ever did Ganymede herself. Yet, notwithstanding this readiness to serve the visitors in their gastronomic desires, the poor steward felt ill-requited; he was twice frightened into an icicle, and twice thawed back into conscious horror, by the rudeness of those he entertained. In one instance, when he had filled out a sparkling glass for a ruffian, and believed he had quite won the heart of the drinker by the act, he found himself grasped roughly and tightly by the throat, and the point of a knife staring him in the face. It seems the fellow who thus seized him, had felt between his teeth a sharp bit of broken glass, and fancying that something had been put in the wine to poison him, he determined to prove his suspicions by making the steward swallow what remained in the bottle from which the liquor had been drawn, and thus unceremoniously prefaced his command; however, ready and implicit obedience averted further bad consequences. The other instance of the steward's jeopardy was this; when the repast was ended, one of the gentlemen coolly requested him to waive all delicacy, and point out the place in which the captain's money was concealed. He might as well have asked him to produce the philosopher's stone. However, pleading the truth was of no use; his determined requisitor seconded the demand by snapping a pistol at his breast; having missed fire, he recocked, and again presented, but the fatal weapon was struck aside by Barbazan, who reproved the rashness with a threat, and thus averted the steward's impending fate. It was then with feelings of satisfaction he heard himself ordered to go down to the hold, and in a moment he was bolted in among his fellow sufferers.

The ruffians indulged in the pleasures of the bottle for some time longer, and then having ordered down the females, treated them with even less humanity than characterized their conduct towards the others. The screams of the helpless females were heard in the hold by those who were unable to render them assistance, and agonizing, indeed, must those screams have been to their incarcerated hearers! How far the brutality of the pirates was carried in this stage of the horrid proceeding, we can only surmise; fortunately, their lives were spared, although, as it afterwards appeared, the orders of Soto were to butcher every being on board; and it is thought that these orders were not put into action, in consequence of the villains having wasted so much time in drinking, and otherwise indulging themselves; for it was not until the loud voice of their chief was heard to recall them, that they prepared to leave the ship; they therefore contented themselves with fastening the women within the cabin, heaping heavy lumber on the hatches of the hold, and boring holes in the planks of the vessel below the surface of the water, so that in destroying the unhappy people at one swoop, they might make up for the lost time. They then left the ship, sinking fast to her apparently certain fate.

It may be reasonably supposed, bad as their conduct was towards the females, and pitiable as was the suffering it produced, that the lives of the whole left to perish were preserved through it; for the ship must have gone down if the women had been either taken out of her or murdered, and those in the hold inevitably have gone with her to the bottom. But by good fortune, the females succeeded in forcing their way out of the cabin, and became the means of liberating the men confined in the hold. When they came on deck, it was nearly dark, yet they could see the pirate ship at a considerable distance, with all her sails set and bearing away from them. They prudently waited, concealed from the possibility of being seen by the enemy, and when the night fell, they crept to the hatchway, and called out to the men below to endeavor to effect their liberation, informing them that the pirate was away and out of sight. They then united their efforts, and the lumber being removed, the hatches gave way to the force below, so that the released captives breathed of hope again. The delightful draught, however, was checked, when the ship was found to contain six feet of water! A momentary collapse took possession of all their newly excited expectations; cries and groans of despair burst forth, but the sailors energy quickly returned, and was followed by that of the others; they set to work at the pumps, and by dint of labor succeeded in keeping the vessel afloat. Yet to direct her course was impossible; the pirates having completely disabled her, by cutting away her rigging and sawing the masts all the way through. The eye of Providence, however, was not averted from the hapless people, for they fell in with a vessel next day that relieved them from their distressing situation, and brought them to England in safety.

We will now return to Soto, and show how the hand of that Providence that secured his intended victims, fell upon himself and his wicked associates. Intoxicated with their infamous success, the night had far advanced before Soto learned that the people in the *Morning*

Star, instead of being slaughtered, were only left to be drowned. The information excited his utmost rage. He reproached Barbazan, and

those who had accompanied them in the boarding, with disobeying his orders, and declared that now there could be no security for their lives. Late as the hour was, and long as he had been steering away from the *Morning Star*, he determined to put back, in the hope of effectually preventing the escape of those in the devoted vessel, by seeing them destroyed before his eyes. Soto was a follower of the principle inculcated by the old maxim, "Dead men tell no tales;" and in pursuance of his doctrine, lost not a moment in putting about and running back. But it was too late; he could find no trace of the vessel, and so consoled himself with the belief that she was at the bottom of the sea, many fathoms below the ken and cognizance of Admiralty Courts.

Soto, thus satisfied, bent his course to Europe. On his voyage he fell in with a small brig, boarded, plundered, sunk her, and, that he might not again run the hazard of encountering living witnesses of his guilt, murdered the crew, with the exception of one individual, whom he took along with him, on account of his knowledge of the course to Corunna, whither he intended to proceed. But, faithful to his principles of self-protection, as soon as he had made full use of the unfortunate sailor, and found himself in sight of the destined port, he came up to him at the helm, which he held in his hand, "My friend," said he "is that the harbor of Corunna?"—"Yes," was the reply. "Then," rejoined Soto, "You have done your duty well, and I am obliged to you for your services." On the instant he drew a pistol and shot the man; then coolly flung his body overboard, took the helm himself, and steered into his native harbor as little concerned as if he had returned from an honest voyage. At this port he obtained papers in a false name, disposed of a great part of his booty, and after a short stay set out for Cadiz, where he expected a market for the remainder. He had a fair wind until he came within sight of the coast near that city. It was coming on dark and he lay to, expecting to go into his anchorage next morning, but the wind shifted to the westward, and suddenly began to blow a heavy gale; it was right on the land. He luffed his ship as close to the wind as possible, in order to clear a point that stretched outward, and beat off to windward, but his leeway carried him towards the land, and he was caught when he least expected the trap. The gale increased—the night grew pitchy dark—the roaring breakers were on his lee beam—the drifting vessel strikes, rebounds, and strikes again—the cry of horror rings through the flapping cordage, and despair is in the eyes of the demon crew. Helpless they lie amid the wrath of the storm, and the darkened face of Heaven, for the first time, strikes terror on their guilty hearts. Death is before them, but not with a merciful quickness does he approach; hour after hour the

frightful vision glares upon them, and at length disappears only to come upon them again in a more dreadful form. The tempest abates, and the sinners were spared for the time.

As the daylight broke they took to their boats, and abandoned the vessel to preserve their lives. But there was no repentance in the pirates; along with the night and the winds went the voice of conscience, and they thought no more of what had passed. They stood upon the beach gazing at the wreck, and the first thought of Soto was to sell it, and purchase another vessel for the renewal of his atrocious pursuits. With the marked decision of his character, he proposed his intention to his followers, and received their full approbation. The plan was instantly arranged; they were to present themselves as honest, shipwrecked mariners to the authorities at Cadiz; Soto was to take upon himself the office of mate, or contra maestra, to an imaginary captain, and thus obtain their sanction in disposing of the vessel. In their assumed character, the whole proceeded to Cadiz, and presented themselves before the proper officers of the marine. Their story was listened to with sympathy, and for a few days every thing went on to their satisfaction. Soto had succeeded so well as to conclude the sale of the wreck with a broker, for the sum of one thousand seven hundred and fifty dollars; the contract was signed, but fortunately the money was not yet paid, when suspicion arose, from some inconsistencies in the pirates account of themselves, and six of them were arrested by the authorities. Soto and one of his crew instantly disappeared from Cadiz, and succeeded in arriving at the neutral ground before Gibraltar, and six more made their escape to the Carraccas.

None are permitted to enter the fortress of Gibraltar, without permission from the governor, or a passport. Soto and his companion, therefore, took up their quarters at a posada on the neutral ground, and resided there in security for several days. The busy and daring mind of the former could not long remain inactive; he proposed to his companion to attempt to enter the garrison in disguise and by stealth, but could not prevail upon him to consent. He therefore resolved to go in alone; and his object in doing so was to procure a supply of money by a letter of credit that he brought with him from Cadiz. His companion, more wise than he, chose the safer course; he knew that the neutral ground was not much controllable by the laws either of the Spanish or the English, and although there was not much probability of being discovered, he resolved not to trust to chance in so great a stake as his life; and he proved to have been right in his judgment, for had he gone to Gibraltar, he would have shared the same fate of his chief. This man is the only one of the whole gang, who has not met with the punishment of his crimes, for he succeeded in effecting his escape on board some vessel. It is not even suspected to what country he is gone; but his description, no doubt, is registered. The steward of the *Morning Star* informed me, that he is a tall, stout man, with fair hair, and fresh complexion, of a mild and gentle countenance, but that he was one of the worst villains of the whole piratical crew. I believe he is stated to be a Frenchman.

Soto secured his admission into the garrison by a false pass, and took up his residence at an inferior tavern in a narrow lane, which runs off the main street of Gibraltar, and is kept by a man of the name of Basso. The appearance of this house suits well with the associations of the worthy Benito's life. I have occasion to pass the door frequently at night, for our barrack (the Casement), is but a few yards from it. I never look at the place without feeling an involuntary sensation of horror: the smoky and dirty nooks;—the distant groups of dark Spaniards, Moors, and Jews, their sallow countenances made yellow by the fight of dim oil lamps; the unceiled rafters of the rooms above, seen through unshuttered windows, and the consciousness of their having covered the atrocious Soto combine this effect upon me.

In this den the villain remained for a few weeks, and during this time seemed to enjoy himself as if he had never committed a murder. The story he told Basso of his circumstances was that he had come to Gibraltar on his way to Cadiz from Malaga, and was merely awaiting the arrival of a friend. He dressed expensively—generally wore a white hat of the best English quality, silk stockings, white trowsers, and blue frock coat. His whiskers were large and bushy, and his hair, which was very black, profuse, long and naturally curled, was much in the style of a London preacher of prophetic and antipoetic notoriety. He was deeply browned with the sun, and had an air and gait expressive of his bold, enterprising, and desperate mind. Indeed, when I saw him in his cell and at his trial, although his frame was attenuated almost to a skeleton, the color of his face a pale yellow, his eyes sunken, and hair closely shorn, he still exhibited strong traces of what he had been, still retained his erect and fearless carriage, his quick, fiery, and malevolent eye, his hurried and concise speech, and his close and pertinent style of remark. He appeared to me such a man as would have made a hero in the ranks of his country, had circumstances placed him in the proper road to fame; but ignorance and poverty turned into the most ferocious robber, one who might have rendered service and been an honor to his sunken country. I should like to hear what the phrenologists say of his head; it appeared to me to be the most peculiar I had ever seen, and certainly, as far as the bump of destructiveness went, bore the theory fully out. It is rumored here that the skull has been sent to the savans of Edinburg; if this be the case, we shall no doubt be made acquainted with their sage opinions upon the subject, and great conquerors will receive a farther assurance of how much they resemble in their physical natures the greatest murderers.

When I visited the pirate in the Moorish castle where he was confined, he was sitting in his cold, narrow, and miserable cell, upon a pallet of straw, eating his coarse meal from a tin plate. I thought him more an object of pity than vengeance; he looked so worn with disease, so crushed with suffering, yet so affable, frank, and kind in his address; for he happened to be in a communicative mood, a thing that was by no means common with him. He spoke of his long confinement, till I thought the tears were about to start from his eyes, and alluded to his approaching trial with satisfaction; but his predominant characteristic, ferocity, appeared in his small piercing black eyes before I left him, as he alluded to his keeper, the Provost, in such a way that made me suspect his desire for blood was not yet extinguished. When he appeared in court on his trial, his demeanor was quite altered; he seemed to me to have suddenly risen out of the wretch he was in his cell, to all the qualities I had heard of him; he stood erect and unembarrassed; he spoke with a strong voice, attended closely to the proceedings, occasionally examined the witnesses, and at the conclusion protested against the justice of his trial. He sometimes spoke to the guards around him, and sometimes affected an air of carelessness of his awful situation, which, however, did not sit easy upon him. Even here the leading trait of his mind broke forth; for when the interpreter commenced his office, the language that he made use of being pedantic and affected, Soto interrupted him thus, while a scowl sat upon his brow that terrified the man of words: "I don't understand you, man; speak Spanish like others, and I'll listen to you." When the dirk that belonged to Mr. Robertson, the trunk and clothes taken from Mr. Gibson, and the pocket book containing the ill-fated captain's handwriting were placed before him, and proved to have been found in his room; and when the maid servant of the tavern proved that she found the dirk under his pillow every morning on arranging his bed; and when he was confronted with his own black slave, between two wax lights, the countenance of the villain appeared in its true nature, not depressed nor sorrowful, but vivid and ferocious; and when the patient and dignified governor, Sir George Don, passed the just sentence of the law upon him, he looked daggers at his heart, and assumed a horrid silence, more eloquent than words.

The criminal persisted up to the day before his execution in asserting his innocence, and inveighing against the injustice of his trial, but the certainty of his fate, and the awful voice of religion, at length subdued him. He made an unreserved confession of his guilt, and became truly penitent, gave up to the keeper the blade of a razor which he had secreted between the soles of his shoes for the acknowledged purpose of adding suicide to his crimes, and seemed to wish for the moment that was to send him before his Creator.

I witnessed his execution, and I believe there never was a more contrite man than he appeared to be; yet there were no driveling fears upon him—he walked firmly at the tail of the fatal cart, gazing sometimes at his coffin, sometimes at the crucifix that he held in his hand. The symbol of divinity he frequently pressed to his lips, repeated the

prayers spoken in his ear by the attendant clergyman, and seemed regardless of every thing but the world to come. The gallows was erected
beside the water, and fronting the neutral ground. He mounted the cart
as firmly as he had walked behind it, and held up his face to Heaven
and the beating rain, calm, resigned, but unshaken; and finding the
halter too high for his neck, he boldly stepped upon his coffin, and
placed his head in the noose, then watching the first turn of the wheels,
he murmured "adios todos" ["Farewell, all"] and leaned forward to fa-
cilitate his fall.

The black slave of the pirate stood upon the battery trembling before
his dying master to behold the awful termination of a series of events, the
recital of which to his African countrymen, when he shall return to his
home, will give them no doubt, a dreadful picture of European civiliza-
tion. The black boy was acquitted at Cadiz, but the men who had fled to
the Carraccas, as well as those arrested after the wreck, were convicted,
executed, their limbs severed, and hung on tenter hooks, as a warning to
all pirates. ☾

chapter 7

Blueskin the Pirate

BY HOWARD PYLE

Cape May and Cape Henlopen form, as it were, the upper and lower jaws of a gigantic mouth, which disgorges from its monstrous gullet the cloudy waters of the Delaware Bay into the heaving, sparkling blue-green of the Atlantic Ocean. From Cape Henlopen as the lower jaw there juts out a long, curving fang of high, smooth-rolling sand dunes, cutting sharp and clean against the still, blue sky above silent, naked, utterly deserted, excepting for the squat, white-walled lighthouse standing upon the crest of the highest hill. Within this curving, sheltering hook of sand hills lie the smooth waters of Lewes Harbor, and, set a little back from the shore, the quaint old town, with its dingy wooden houses of clapboard and shingle, looks sleepily out through the masts of the shipping lying at anchor in the harbor, to the purple, clean-cut, level thread of the ocean horizon beyond.

Lewes is a queer, odd, old-fashioned little town, smelling fragrant of salt marsh and sea breeze. It is rarely visited by strangers. The people who live there are the progeny of people who have lived there for many generations, and it is the very place to nurse, and preserve, and care for old legends and traditions of bygone times, until they grow from bits of gossip and news into local history of considerable size. As in the busier world men talk of last year's elections, here these old bits, and scraps, and odds and ends of history are retailed to the listener who cares to listen—traditions of the War of 1812, when Beresford's fleet lay off the harbor threatening to bombard the town; tales of the Revolution and of Earl Howe's warships, tarrying for a while in the quiet harbor before they sailed up the river to shake old Philadelphia town with the thunders of their guns at Red Bank and Fort Mifflin.

With these substantial and sober threads of real history, other and more lurid colors are interwoven into the web of local lore—legends of the dark doings of famous pirates, of their mysterious, sinister comings and goings, of treasures buried in the sand dunes and pine barrens back of the cape and along the Atlantic beach to the southward.

Of such is the story of Blueskin, the pirate.

It was in the fall and the early winter of the year 1750, and again in the summer of the year following, that the famous pirate, Blueskin, became especially identified with Lewes as a part of its traditional history.

For some time—for three or four years—rumors and reports of Blueskin's doings in the West Indies and off the Carolinas had been brought in now and then by sea captains. There was no more cruel, bloody, desperate, devilish pirate than he in all those pirate-infested waters. All kinds of wild and bloody stories were current concerning him, but it never occurred to the good folk of Lewes that such stories were some time to be a part of their own history.

But one day a schooner came drifting into Lewes harbor—shattered, wounded, her forecastle splintered, her foremast shot half away, and three great tattered holes in her mainsail. The mate with one of the crew came ashore in the boat for help and a doctor. He reported that the captain and the cook were dead and there were three wounded men aboard. The story he told to the gathering crowd brought a very peculiar thrill to those who heard it. They had fallen in with Blueskin, he said, off Fenwick's Island (some twenty or thirty miles below the capes), and the pirates had come aboard of them; but, finding that the cargo of the schooner consisted only of cypress shingles and lumber, had soon quitted their prize. Perhaps Blueskin was disappointed at not finding a more valuable capture; perhaps the spirit of deviltry was hotter in him that morning than usual; anyhow, as the pirate craft bore away she fired three broadsides at short range into the helpless coaster. The captain had been killed at the first fire, the cook had died on the way up, three of the crew were wounded, and the vessel was leaking fast, betwixt wind and water.

Such was the mate's story. It spread like wildfire, and in half an hour all the town was in a ferment. Fenwick's Island was very near home; Blueskin might come sailing into the harbor at any minute and then—! In an hour Sheriff Jones had called together most of the able-bodied men of the town, muskets and rifles were taken down from the chimney places, and every preparation was made to defend the place against the pirates, should they come into the harbor and attempt to land.

But Blueskin did not come that day, nor did he come the next or the next. But on the afternoon of the third the news went suddenly flying over the town that the pirates were inside the capes. As the report spread the people came running—men, women, and children—to the green before the tavern, where a little knot of old seamen were gathered together, looking fixedly out toward the offing, talking in low voices. Two vessels, one bark-rigged, the other and smaller a sloop, were slowly creeping up the bay, a couple of miles or so away and just inside the cape. There appeared nothing remarkable about the two crafts, but the little crowd that continued gathering upon the green stood looking out across the bay at them none the less anxiously for that. They were sailing close-hauled to the wind, the sloop following in the wake of her consort as the pilot fish follows in the wake of the shark.

But the course they held did not lie toward the harbor, but rather bore away toward the Jersey shore, and by and by it began to be apparent that Blueskin did not intend visiting the town. Nevertheless, those who stood looking did not draw a free breath until, after watching the two pirates for more than an hour and a half, they saw them—then about six miles away—suddenly put about and sail with a free wind out to sea again.

"The bloody villains have gone!" said old Captain Wolfe, shutting his telescope with a click.

But Lewes was not yet quit of Blueskin. Two days later a half-breed from Indian River bay came up, bringing the news that the pirates had sailed into the inlet—some fifteen miles below Lewes—and had careened the bark to clean her.

Perhaps Blueskin did not care to stir up the country people against him, for the half-breed reported that the pirates were doing no harm, and that what they took from the farmers of Indian River and Rehoboth they paid for with good hard money.

It was while the excitement over the pirates was at its highest fever heat that Levi West came home again.

Even in the middle of the last century the grist mill, a couple of miles from Lewes, although it was at most but fifty or sixty years old, had all a look of weather-beaten age, for the cypress shingles, of which it was built, ripen in a few years of wind and weather to a silvery, hoary gray, and the white powdering of flour lent it a look as though the dust of ages had settled upon it, making the shadows within dim, soft, mysterious. A dozen willow trees shaded with dappling, shivering ripples of shadow the road before the mill door, and the mill itself, and the long, narrow, shingle-built, one-storied, hip-roofed dwelling house. At the time of the story the mill had descended in a direct line of succession to Hiram White, the grandson of old Ephraim White, who had built it, it was said, in 1701.

Hiram White was only twenty-seven years old, but he was already in local repute as a "character." As a boy he was thought to be half-witted or "natural," and, as is the case with such unfortunates in small country towns where everybody knows everybody, he was made a common sport and jest for the keener, crueler wits of the neighborhood. Now that he was grown to the ripeness of manhood he was still looked upon as being—to use a quaint expression—"slack," or "not jest right." He was heavy, awkward, ungainly and loose-jointed, and enormously, prodigiously strong. He had a lumpish, thick-featured face, with lips heavy and loosely hanging, that gave him an air of stupidity, half droll, half pathetic. His little eyes were set far apart and flat with his face, his eyebrows were nearly white and his hair was of a sandy, colorless kind. He was singularly taciturn, lisping thickly when he did talk, and stuttering and hesitating in his speech, as though his words moved faster than his mind could follow. It was the custom for local wags to urge, or badger, or tempt him to talk, for the sake of the ready laugh that always followed the few thick, stammering words and the stupid drooping of the jaw at the end of each short speech. Perhaps Squire Hall was the only one in Lewes Hundred who misdoubted that Hiram was half-witted. He had had dealings with him and was wont to say that whoever bought Hiram White for a fool made a fool's bargain. Certainly, whether he had common wits or no, Hiram had managed his mill to pretty good purpose and was fairly well off in the world as prosperity went in southern Delaware and in those days. No doubt, had it come to the pinch, he might have bought some of his tormentors out three times over.

Hiram White had suffered quite a financial loss some six months before, through that very Blueskin who was now lurking in Indian River inlet. He had entered into a "venture" with Josiah Shippin, a Philadelphia merchant, to the tune of seven hundred pounds sterling. The money had been invested in a cargo of flour and corn meal that had been shipped to Jamaica by the bark *Nancy Lee*. The *Nancy Lee* had been captured by the pirates off Currituck Sound, the crew set adrift in the longboat, and the bark herself and all her cargo burned to the water's edge.

Five hundred of the seven hundred pounds invested in the unfortunate "venture" was money bequeathed by Hiram's father, seven years before, to Levi West.

Eleazer White had been twice married, the second time to the widow West. She had brought with her to her new home a good-looking, long-legged, black-eyed, black-haired ne'er-do-well of a son, a year or so younger than Hiram. He was a shrewd, quick-witted lad, idle, shiftless, willful, ill-trained perhaps, but as bright and keen as a pin. He was the very opposite to poor, dull Hiram. Eleazer White had never loved his son; he was ashamed of the poor, slack-witted oaf. Upon the other hand, he was very fond of Levi West, whom he always called "our Levi," and whom he treated in every way as though he were his own son. He tried to train the lad to work in the mill, and was patient beyond what the patience of most fathers would have been with his stepson's idleness and shiftlessness. "Never mind," he was used to say. "Levi'll come all right. Levi's as bright as a button."

It was one of the greatest blows of the old miller's life when Levi ran away to sea. In his last sickness the old man's mind constantly turned to his lost stepson. "Mebby he'll come back again," said he, "and if he does I want you to be good to him, Hiram. I've done my duty by you and have left you the house and mill, but I want you to promise that if Levi comes back again you'll give him a home and a shelter under this roof if he wants one." And Hiram had promised to do as his father asked.

After Eleazer died it was found that he had bequeathed five hundred pounds to his "beloved stepson, Levi West," and had left Squire Hall as trustee.

Levi West had been gone nearly nine years and not a word had been heard from him; there could be little or no doubt that he was dead.

One day Hiram came into Squire Hall's office with a letter in his hand. It was the time of the old French war, and flour and corn meal were fetching fabulous prices in the British West Indies. The letter Hiram brought with him was from a Philadelphia merchant, Josiah Shippin, with whom he had had some dealings. Mr. Shippin proposed that Hiram should join him in sending a "venture" of flour and corn meal to Kingston, Jamaica. Hiram had slept upon the letter overnight and now he brought it to the old Squire. Squire Hall read the letter, shaking his head the while. "Too much risk, Hiram!" said he. "Mr Shippin wouldn't have asked you to go into this venture if he could have got anybody else to do so. My advice is that you let it alone. I reckon you've come to me for advice?" Hiram shook his head. "Ye haven't? What have ye come for, then?"

"Seven hundred pounds," said Hiram.

"Seven hundred pounds!" said Squire Hall. "I haven't got seven hundred pounds to lend you, Hiram."

"Five hundred been left to Levi—I got hundred—raise hundred more on mortgage," said Hiram.

"Tut, tut, Hiram," said Squire Hall, "that'll never do in the world. Suppose Levi West should come back again, what then? I'm responsible for that money. If you wanted to borrow it now for any reasonable venture, you should have it and welcome, but for such a wildcat scheme—"

"Levi never come back," said Hiram—"nine years gone Levi's dead."

"Mebby he is," said Squire Hall, "but we don't know that."

"I'll give bond for security," said Hiram.

Squire Hall thought for a while in silence. "Very well, Hiram," said he by and by, "if you'll do that. Your father left the money, and I don't see that it's right for me to stay his son from using it. But if it is lost, Hiram, and if Levi should come back, it will go well to ruin ye."

So Hiram White invested seven hundred pounds in the Jamaica venture and every farthing of it was burned by Blueskin, off Currituck Sound.

Sally Martin was said to be the prettiest girl in Lewes Hundred, and when the rumor began to leak out that Hiram White was courting her the whole community took it as a monstrous joke. It was the common thing to greet Hiram himself with, "Hey, Hiram, how's Sally?" Hiram never made answer to such salutation, but went his way as heavily, as impassively, as dully as ever.

The joke was true. Twice a week, rain or shine, Hiram White never failed to scrape his feet upon Billy Martin's doorstep. Twice a week, on Sundays and Thursdays, he never failed to take his customary seat by the kitchen fire. He rarely said anything by way of talk; he nodded to the farmer, to his wife, to Sally and, when he chanced to be at home, to her brother, but he ventured nothing further. There he would sit from half past seven until nine o'clock, stolid, heavy, impassive, his dull eyes following now one of the family and now another, but always coming back again to Sally. It sometimes happened that she had other company—some of the young men of the neighborhood. The presence of such seemed to make no difference to Hiram; he bore whatever broad jokes might be cracked upon him, whatever grins, whatever giggling might follow those jokes, with the same patient impassiveness. There he would sit, silent, unresponsive; then, at the first stroke of nine o'clock, he would rise, shoulder his ungainly person into his overcoat, twist his head into his three-cornered hat, and with a "Good night, Sally, I be going now," would take his departure, shutting the door carefully to behind him.

Never, perhaps, was there a girl in the world had such a lover and such a courtship as Sally Martin.

It was one Thursday evening in the latter part of November, about a week after Blueskin's appearance off the capes, and while the one subject of talk was of the pirates being in Indian River inlet. The air was still and wintry; a sudden cold snap had set in and skims of ice had formed over puddles in the road; the smoke from the chimneys rose straight in the quiet air and voices sounded loud, as they do in frosty weather.

Hiram White sat by the dim light of a tallow dip, pouring laboriously over some account books. It was not quite seven o'clock, and he never started for Billy Martin's before that hour. As he ran his finger slowly and hesitatingly down the column of figures, he heard the kitchen door beyond open and shut, the noise of footsteps crossing the floor and the scraping of a chair dragged forward to the hearth. Then came the sound of a basket of corncobs being emptied on the smoldering blaze and then the snapping and crackling of the reanimated fire. Hiram thought nothing of all this, excepting, in a dim sort of way, that it was Bob, the Negro mill hand, or old black Dinah, the housekeeper, and so went on with his calculations.

At last he closed the books with a snap and, smoothing down his hair, arose, took up the candle, and passed out of the room into the kitchen beyond.

A man was sitting in front of the corncob fire that flamed and blazed in the great, gaping, sooty fireplace. A rough overcoat was flung over the chair behind him and his hands were spread out to the roaring warmth. At the sound of the lifted latch and of Hiram's entrance he turned his head, and when Hiram saw his face he stood suddenly still as though turned to stone. The face, marvelously altered and changed as it was, was the face of his stepbrother, Levi West. He was not dead; he had come home again. For a time not a sound broke the dead, unbroken silence excepting the crackling of the blaze in the fireplace and the sharp ticking of the tall clock in the corner. The one face, dull and stolid, with the light of the candle shining upward over its lumpy features, looked fixedly, immovably, stonily at the other, sharp, shrewd, cunning—the red wavering light of the blaze shining upon the high cheek bones, cutting sharp on the nose and twinkling in the glassy turn of the black, ratlike eyes. Then suddenly that face cracked, broadened, spread to a grin. "I have come back again, Hi," said Levi, and at the sound of the words the speechless spell was broken.

Hiram answered never a word, but he walked to the fireplace, set the candle down upon the dusty mantelshelf among the boxes and bottles, and, drawing forward a chair upon the other side of the hearth, sat down.

His dull little eyes never moved from his stepbrother's face. There was no curiosity in his expression, no surprise, no wonder. The heavy under lip dropped a little farther open and there was more than usual of dull, expressionless stupidity upon the lumpish face; but that was all.

As was said, the face upon which he looked was strangely, marvelously changed from what it had been when he had last seen it nine years before, and, though it was still the face of Levi West, it was a very different Levi West than the shiftless ne'er-do-well who had run away to sea in the Brazilian brig that long time ago. That Levi West had been a rough, careless, happy-go-lucky fellow, thoughtless and selfish, but with nothing essentially evil or sinister in his nature. The Levi West that now sat in a rush-bottom chair at the other side of the fireplace had that stamped upon his front that might be both evil and sinister. His swart complexion was tanned to an Indian copper. On one side of his face was a curious discoloration in the skin and a long, crooked, cruel scar that ran diagonally across forehead and temple and cheek in a white, jagged seam. This discoloration was of a livid blue, about the tint of a tattoo mark. It made a patch the size of a man's hand, lying across the cheek and the side of the neck. Hiram could not keep his eyes from this mark and the white scar cutting across it.

There was an odd sort of incongruity in Levi's dress; a pair of heavy gold earrings and a dirty red handkerchief knotted loosely around his neck, beneath an open collar, displaying to its full length the lean, sinewy throat with its bony "Adam's apple," gave to his costume somewhat the smack of a sailor. He wore a coat that had once been of fine plum color—now stained and faded—too small for his lean length, and furbished with tarnished lace. Dirty cambric cuffs hung at his wrists and on his fingers were half a dozen and more rings, set with stones that shone, and glistened, and twinkled in the light of the fire. The hair at either temple was twisted into a Spanish curl, plastered flat to the cheek, and a plaited queue hung halfway down his back.

Hiram, speaking never a word, sat motionless, his dull little eyes traveling slowly up and down and around and around his stepbrother's person.

Levi did not seem to notice his scrutiny, leaning forward, now with his palms spread out to the grateful warmth, now rubbing them slowly together. But at last he suddenly whirled his chair around, rasping on the floor, and faced his stepbrother. He thrust his hand into his capacious coat pocket and brought out a pipe which he proceeded to fill from a skin of tobacco. "Well, Hi," said he, "d'ye see I've come back home again?"

"Thought you was dead," said Hiram, dully.

Levi laughed, then he drew a red-hot coal out of the fire, put it upon the bowl of the pipe, and began puffing out clouds of pungent smoke. "Nay, nay," said he, "not dead—not dead by odds. But [puff] by the Eternal Holy, Hi, I played many a close game [puff] with old Davy Jones, for all that."

Hiram's look turned inquiringly toward the jagged scar and Levi caught the slow glance. "You're lookin' at this," said he, running his finger down the crooked seam. "That looks bad, but it wasn't so close as this"—laying his hand for a moment upon the livid stain. "A cooly devil off Singapore gave me that cut when we fell foul of an opium junk in the China Sea four years ago last September. This," touching the disfiguring blue patch again, "was a closer miss, Hi. A Spanish captain fired a pistol at me down off Santa Catharina. He was so nigh that the powder went under the skin and it'll never come out again—his eyes—he had better have fired the pistol into his own head that morning. But never mind that. I reckon I'm changed, ain't I, Hi?"

He took his pipe out of his mouth and looked inquiringly at Hiram, who nodded.

Levi laughed. "Devil doubt it," said he, "but whether I'm changed or no, I'll take my affidavy that you are the same old half-witted Hi that you used to be. I remember dad used to say that you hadn't no more than enough wits to keep you out of the rain. And, talking of dad, Hi, I hearn tell he's been dead now these nine years gone. D'ye know what I've come home for?"

Hiram shook his head.

"I've come for that five hundred pounds that dad left me when he died, for I hearn tell of that, too."

Hiram sat quite still for a second or two and then he said, "I put that money out to venture and lost it all."

Levi's face fell and he took his pipe out of his mouth, regarding Hiram sharply and keenly. "What d'ye mean?" said he presently.

"I thought you was dead—and I put—seven hundred pounds—into *Nancy Lee*—and Blueskin burned her—off Currituck."

"Burned her off Currituck!" repeated Levi. Then suddenly a light seemed to break upon his comprehension. "Burned by Blueskin!" he repeated, and thereupon flung himself back in his chair and burst into a short, boisterous fit of laughter. "Well, by the Holy Eternal, Hi, if that isn't a piece of your tarnal luck. Burned by Blueskin, was it?" He paused for a moment, as though turning it over in his mind. Then he laughed again. "All the same," said he presently, "d'ye see, I can't suffer for Blueskin's doings. The money was willed to me, fair and true, and you have got to pay it, Hiram White, burn or sink, Blueskin or no Blueskin." Again he puffed for a moment or two in reflective silence. "All the same, Hi," said he, once more resuming the thread of talk, "I don't reckon to be too hard on you. You be only half-witted, anyway, and I sha'n't be too hard on you. I give you a month to raise that money, and while you're doing it I'll jest hang around here. I've been in trouble, Hi, d'ye see. I'm under a cloud and so I want to keep here, as quiet as may be. I'll tell ye how it came about: I had a set-to with a land pirate in Philadelphia, and somebody got hurt. That's the reason I'm here now, and don't you say anything about it. Do you understand?"

Hiram opened his lips as though it was his intent to answer, then seemed to think better of it and contented himself by nodding his head.

That Thursday night was the first for a six-month that Hiram White did not scrape his feet clean at Billy Martin's doorstep.

Within a week Levi West had pretty well established himself among his old friends and acquaintances, though upon a different footing from that of nine years before, for this was a very different Levi from that other. Nevertheless, he was none the less popular in the barroom of the tavern and at the country store, where he was always the center of a group of loungers. His nine years seemed to have been crowded full of the wildest of wild adventures and happenings, as well by land as by sea, and, given an appreciative audience, he would reel off his yarns by the hour, in a reckless, devil-may-care fashion that set agape even old sea dogs who had sailed the western ocean since boyhood. Then he seemed always to have plenty of money, and he loved to spend it at the tavern taproom, with a lavishness that was at once the wonder and admiration of gossips.

At that time, as was said, Blueskin was the one engrossing topic of talk, and it added not a little to Levi's prestige when it was found that he had actually often seen that bloody, devilish pirate with his own eyes. A great, heavy, burly fellow, Levi said he was, with a beard as black as a hat— a devil with his sword and pistol afloat, but not so black as he was painted when ashore. He told of many adventures in which Blueskin figured and was then always listened to with more than usual gaping interest.

As for Blueskin, the quiet way in which the pirates conducted them- selves at Indian River almost made the Lewes folk forget what he could do when the occasion called. They almost ceased to remember that poor shattered schooner that had crawled with its ghastly dead and groaning wounded into the harbor a couple of weeks since. But if for a while they forgot who or what Blueskin was, it was not for long.

One day a bark from Bristol, bound for Cuba and laden with a valuable cargo of cloth stuffs and silks, put into Lewes harbor to take in water. The captain himself came ashore and was at the tavern for two or three hours. It happened that Levi was there and that the talk was of Blueskin. The English captain, a grizzled old sea dog, listened to Levi's yarns with not a little contempt. He had, he said, sailed in the China Sea and the Indian Ocean too long to be afraid of any hog-eating Yankee pirate such as this Blueskin. A junk full of coolies armed with stinkpots was something to speak of, but who ever heard of the likes of Blueskin falling afoul of anything more than a Spanish canoe or a Yankee coaster?

Levi grinned. "All the same, my hearty," said he, "if I was you I'd give Blueskin a wide berth. I hear that he's cleaned the vessel that was careened awhile ago, and mebby he'll give you a little trouble if you come too nigh him."

To this the Englishman only answered that Blueskin might be——, and that the next afternoon, wind and weather permitting, he intended to heave anchor and run out to sea.

Levi laughed again. "I wish I might be here to see what'll happen," said he, "but I'm going up the river tonight to see a gal and mebby won't be back again for three or four days."

The next afternoon the English bark set sail as the captain promised, and that night Lewes town was awake until almost morning, gazing at a broad red glare that lighted up the sky away toward the southeast. Two days afterward a Negro oysterman came up from Indian River with news that the pirates were lying off the inlet, bringing ashore bales of goods from their larger vessel and piling the same upon the beach under tarpaulins. He said that it was known down at Indian River that Blueskin had fallen afoul of an English bark, had burned her and had murdered the captain and all but three of the crew, who had joined with the pirates.

The excitement over this terrible happening had only begun to subside when another occurred to cap it. One afternoon a ship's boat, in which were five men and two women, came rowing into Lewes harbor. It was the longboat of the Charleston packet, bound for New York, and was commanded by the first mate. The packet had been attacked and captured by the pirates about ten leagues south by east of Cape Henlopen. The pirates had come aboard of them at night and no resistance had been offered. Perhaps it was that circumstance that saved the lives of all, for no murder or violence had been done. Nevertheless, officers, passengers and crew had been stripped of everything of value and set adrift in the boats and the ship herself had been burned. The longboat had become separated from the others during the night and had sighted Henlopen a little after sunrise.

It may be here said that Squire Hall made out a report of these two occurrences and sent it up to Philadelphia by the mate of the packet. But for some reason it was nearly four weeks before a sloop of war was sent around from New York. In the meanwhile, the pirates had disposed of the booty stored under the tarpaulins on the beach at Indian River inlet, shipping some of it away in two small sloops and sending the rest by wagons somewhere up the country.

Levi had told the English captain that he was going up-country to visit one of his lady friends. He was gone nearly two weeks. Then once more he appeared, as suddenly, as unexpectedly, as he had done when he first returned to Lewes. Hiram was sitting at supper when the door opened and Levi walked in, hanging up his hat behind the door as unconcernedly as though he had only been gone an hour. He was in an ugly, lowering humor and sat himself down at the table without uttering a word, resting his chin upon his clenched fist and glowering fixedly at the corn cake while Dinah fetched him a plate and knife and fork.

His coming seemed to have taken away all of Hiram's appetite. He pushed away his plate and sat staring at his stepbrother, who presently fell to at the bacon and eggs like a famished wolf. Not a word was said until Levi had ended his meal and filled his pipe. "Look'ee, Hiram," said he, as he stooped over the fire and raked out a hot coal. "Look'ee, Hiram! I've been to Philadelphia, d'ye see, a-settlin' up that trouble I told you about when I first come home. D'ye understand? D'ye remember? D'ye get it through your skull?" He looked around over his shoulder, waiting as though for an answer. But getting none, he continued: "I expect two gentlemen here from Philadelphia tonight. They're friends of mine and are coming to talk over the business and ye needn't stay at home, Hi. You can go out somewhere, d'ye understand?" And then he added with a grin, "Ye can go to see Sally."

Hiram pushed back his chair and arose. He leaned with his back against the side of the fireplace. "I'll stay at home," said he presently.

"But I don't want you to stay at home, Hi," said Levi. "We'll have to talk business and I want you to go!"

"I'll stay at home," said Hiram again.

Levi's brow grew as black as thunder. He ground his teeth together and for a moment or two it seemed as though an explosion was coming. But he swallowed his passion with a gulp. "You're a——pig-headed, half-witted fool," said he. Hiram never so much as moved his eyes. "As for you," said Levi, whirling round upon Dinah, who was clearing the table, and glowering balefully upon the old Negress, "you put them things down and git out of here. Don't you come nigh this kitchen again till I tell ye to. If I catch you pryin' around may I be——, eyes and liver, if I don't cut your heart out."

In about half an hour Levi's friends came; the first a little, thin, wizened man with a very foreign look. He was dressed in a rusty black suit and wore gray yarn stockings and shoes with brass buckles. The other

was also plainly a foreigner. He was dressed in sailor fashion, with petticoat breeches of duck, a heavy peajacket, and thick boots, reaching to
the knees. He wore a red sash tied around his waist, and once, as he
pushed back his coat, Hiram saw the glitter of a pistol butt. He was a
powerful, thickset man, low-browed and bull-necked, his cheek, and
chin, and throat closely covered with a stubble of blue-Blackbeard. He
wore a red kerchief tied around his head and over it a cocked hat,
edged with tarnished gilt braid.

Levi himself opened the door to them. He exchanged a few words
outside with his visitors, in a foreign language of which Hiram understood nothing. Neither of the two strangers spoke a word to Hiram: the
little man shot him a sharp look out of the corners of his eyes and the
burly ruffian scowled blackly at him, but beyond that neither vouch-
safed him any regard.

Levi drew to the shutters, shot the bolt in the outer door, and
tilted a chair against the latch of the one that led from the kitchen into
the adjoining room. Then the three worthies seated themselves at the
table which Dinah had half cleared of the supper china, and were
presently deeply engrossed over a packet of papers which the big,
burly man had brought with him in the pocket of his peajacket. The
confabulation was conducted throughout in the same foreign language
that Levi had used when first speaking to them—a language quite un-
intelligible to Hiram's ears. Now and then the murmur of talk would
rise loud and harsh over some disputed point; now and then it would
sink away to whispers.

Twice the tall clock in the corner whirred and sharply struck the
hour, but throughout the whole long consultation Hiram stood silent,
motionless as a stock, his eyes fixed almost unwinkingly upon the three
heads grouped close together around the dim, flickering light of the
candle and the papers scattered upon the table.

Suddenly the talk came to an end, the three heads separated and
the three chairs were pushed back, grating harshly. Levi rose, went to

the closet and brought thence a bottle of Hiram's apple brandy, as coolly as though it belonged to himself. He set three tumblers and a crock of water upon the table and each helped himself liberally.

As the two visitors departed down the road, Levi stood for a while at the open door, looking after the dusky figures until they were swallowed in the darkness. Then he turned, came in, shut the door, shuddered, took a final dose of the apple brandy and went to bed, without, since his first suppressed explosion, having said a single word to Hiram.

Hiram, left alone, stood for a while, silent, motionless as ever, then he looked slowly about him, gave a shake of the shoulders as though to arouse himself, and taking the candle, left the room, shutting the door noiselessly behind him.

This time of Levi West's unwelcome visitation was indeed a time of bitter trouble and tribulation to poor Hiram White. Money was of very different value in those days than it is now, and five hundred pounds was in its way a good round lump—in Sussex County it was almost a fortune. It was a desperate struggle for Hiram to raise the amount of his father's bequest to his stepbrother. Squire Hall, as may have been gathered, had a very warm and friendly feeling for Hiram, believing in him when all others disbelieved; nevertheless, in the matter of money the old man was as hard and as cold as adamant. He would, he said, do all he could to help Hiram, but that five hundred pounds must and should be raised—Hiram must release his security bond. He would loan him, he said, three hundred pounds, taking a mortgage upon the mill. He would have lent him four hundred but that there was already a first mortgage of one hundred pounds upon it, and he would not dare to put more than three hundred more atop of that.

Hiram had a considerable quantity of wheat that he had bought upon speculation and that was then lying idle in a Philadelphia storehouse. This he had sold at public sale and at a very great sacrifice; he realized barely one hundred pounds upon it. The financial horizon looked very black to him; nevertheless, Levi's five hundred pounds was raised, and paid into Squire Hall's hands, and Squire Hall released Hiram's bond.

The business was finally closed on one cold, gray afternoon in the early part of December. As Hiram tore his bond across and then tore it across again and again, Squire Hall pushed back the papers upon his desk and cocked his feet upon its slanting top. "Hiram," said he, abruptly, "Hiram, do you know that Levi West is forever hanging around Billy Martin's house, after that pretty daughter of his?"

So long a space of silence followed the speech that the Squire began to think that Hiram might not have heard him. But Hiram had heard. "No," said he, "I didn't know it."

"Well, he is," said Squire Hall. "It's the talk of the whole neighborhood. The talk's pretty bad, too. D'ye know that they say that she was away from home three days last week, nobody knew where? The fellow's turned her head with his sailor's yarns and his traveler's lies."

Hiram said not a word, but he sat looking at the other in stolid silence. "That stepbrother of yours," continued the old Squire presently, "is a rascal—he is a rascal, Hiram, and I misdoubt he's something worse. I hear he's been seen in some queer places and with queer company of late."

He stopped again, and still Hiram said nothing. "And look'ee, Hiram," the old man resumed, suddenly, "I do hear that you be courtin' the girl, too; is that so?"

"Yes," said Hiram, "I'm courtin' her, too."

"Tut! tut!" said the Squire, "that's a pity, Hiram. I'm afraid your cakes are dough."

After he had left the Squire's office, Hiram stood for a while in the street, bareheaded, his hat in his hand, staring unwinkingly down at the ground at his feet, with stupidly drooping lips and lackluster eyes.

Presently he raised his hand and began slowly smoothing down the sandy shock of hair upon his forehead. At last he aroused himself with a shake, looked dully up and down the street, and then, putting on his hat, turned and walked slowly and heavily away.

The early dusk of the cloudy winter evening was settling fast, for the sky was leaden and threatening. At the outskirts of the town Hiram stopped again and again stood for a while in brooding thought. Then, finally, he turned slowly, not the way that led homeward, but taking the road that led between the bare and withered fields and crooked fences toward Billy Martin's.

It would be hard to say just what it was that led Hiram to seek Billy Martin's house at that time of day—whether it was fate or ill fortune. He could not have chosen a more opportune time to confirm his own undoing. What he saw was the very worst that his heart feared.

Along the road, at a little distance from the house, was a mock-orange hedge, now bare, naked, leafless. As Hiram drew near he heard footsteps approaching and low voices. He drew back into the fence corner and there stood, half sheltered by the stark network of twigs. Two figures passed slowly along the gray of the roadway in the gloaming. One was his stepbrother, the other was Sally Martin. Levi's arm was around her, he was whispering into her ear, and her head rested upon his shoulder.

Hiram stood as still, as breathless, as cold as ice. They stopped upon the side of the road just beyond where he stood. Hiram's eyes never left them. There for some time they talked together in low voices, their words now and then reaching the ears of that silent, breathless listener.

Suddenly there came the clattering of an opening door, and then Betty Martin's voice broke the silence, harshly, shrilly: "Sal!—Sal!—Sally Martin! You, Sally Martin! Come in yere. Where be ye?"

The girl flung her arms around Levi's neck and their lips met in one quick kiss. The next moment she was gone, flying swiftly, silently, down the road past where Hiram stood, stooping as she ran. Levi stood looking after her until she was gone; then he turned and walked away whistling.

His whistling died shrilly into silence in the wintry distance, and then at last Hiram came stumbling out from the hedge. His face had never looked before as it looked then.

Hiram was standing in front of the fire with his hands clasped behind his back. He had not touched the supper on the table. Levi was eating with an appetite. Suddenly he looked over his plate at his stepbrother.

"How about that five hundred pounds, Hiram?" said he. "I gave ye a month to raise it and the month ain't quite up yet, but I'm goin' to leave this here place day after tomorrow—by next day at the furd'st—and I want the money that's mine."

"I paid it to Squire Hall today and he has it fer ye," said Hiram, dully.

Levi laid down his knife and fork with a clatter. "Squire Hall!" said he, "what's Squire Hall got to do with it? Squire Hall didn't have the use of that money. It was you had it and you have got to pay it back to me, and if you don't do it, by G——, I'll have the law on you, sure as you're born."

"Squire Hall's trustee—I ain't your trustee," said Hiram, in the same dull voice.

"I don't know nothing about trustees," said Levi, "or anything about lawyer business, either. What I want to know is, are you going to pay me my money or no?"

"No," said Hiram, "I ain't—Squire Hall'll pay ye; you go to him."

Levi West's face grew purple red. He pushed back, his chair grating harshly. "You—bloody land pirate!" he said, grinding his teeth together. "I see through your tricks. You're up to cheating me out of my money. You know very well that Squire Hall is down on me, hard and bitter— writin' his——reports to Philadelphia and doing all he can to stir up everybody agin me and to bring the bluejackets down on me. I see through your tricks as clear as glass, but ye shatn't trick me. I'll have my money if there's law in the land—ye bloody, unnatural thief ye, who'd go agin our dead father's will!"

Then—if the roof had fallen in upon him, Levi West could not have been more amazed—Hiram suddenly strode forward, and, leaning half across the table with his fists clenched, fairly glared into Levi's eyes. His face, dull, stupid, wooden, was now fairly convulsed with passion. The great veins stood out upon his temples like knotted whipcords, and when he spoke his voice was more a breathless snarl than the voice of a Christian man.

"Ye'll have the law, will ye?" said he. "Ye'll—have the law, will ye? You're afeared to go to law—Levi West—you try th' law—and see how ye like it. Who're you to call me thief—ye bloody, murderin' villain ye! You're the thief—Levi West—you come here and stole my daddy from me ye did. You make me ruin—myself to pay what oughter to been mine then—ye ye steal the gal I was courtin', to boot." He stopped and his lips rithed for words to say. "I know ye," said he, grinding his teeth. "I know ye! And only for what my daddy made me promise I'd a-had you up to the magistrate's before this."

Then, pointing with quivering finger: "There's the door—you see it! Go out that there door and don't never come into it again—if ye do— or if ye ever come where I can lay eyes on ye again—by th' Holy Holy I'll hale ye up to the Squire's office and tell all I know and all I've seen. Oh, I'll give ye your belly-fill of law if—ye want th' law! Git out of the house, I say!"

As Hiram spoke Levi seemed to shrink together. His face changed from its copper color to a dull, waxy yellow. When the other ended he answered never a word. But he pushed back his chair, rose, put on his hat and, with a furtive, sidelong look, left the house, without stopping to finish the supper that he had begun. He never entered Hiram White's door again.

Hiram had driven out the evil spirit from his home, but the mischief that it had brewed was done and could not be undone. The next day it was known that Sally Martin had run away from home, and that she had run away with Levi West. Old Billy Martin had been in town in the morning with his rifle, hunting for Levi and threatening if he caught him to have his life for leading his daughter astray.

And, as the evil spirit had left Hiram's house, so had another and a greater evil spirit quitted its harborage. It was heard from Indian River in a few days more that Blueskin had quitted the inlet and had sailed away to the southeast; and it was reported, by those who seemed to know, that he had finally quitted those parts.

It was well for himself that Blueskin left when he did, for not three days after he sailed away the *Scorpion* sloop-of-war dropped anchor in Lewes harbor. The New York agent of the unfortunate packet and a government commissioner had also come aboard the *Scorpion*.

Without loss of time, the officer in command instituted a keen and searching examination that brought to light some singularly curious facts. It was found that a very friendly understanding must have existed for some time between the pirates and the people of Indian River, for, in the houses throughout that section, many things—some of considerable value—that had been taken by the pirates from the packet, were discovered and seized by the commissioner. Valuables of a suspicious nature had found their way even into the houses of Lewes itself.

The whole neighborhood seemed to have become more or less tainted by the presence of the pirates.

Even poor Hiram White did not escape the suspicions of having had dealings with them. Of course the examiners were not slow in discovering that Levi West had been deeply concerned with Blueskin's doings.

Old Dinah and black Bob were examined, and not only did the story of Levi's two visitors come to light, but also the fact that Hiram was present and with them while they were in the house disposing of the captured goods to their agent.

Of all that he had endured, nothing seemed to cut poor Hiram so deeply and keenly as these unjust suspicions. They seemed to bring the last bitter pang, hardest of all to bear.

Levi had taken from him his father's love; he had driven him, if not to ruin, at least perilously close to it. He had run away with the girl he loved, and now, through him, even Hiram's good name was gone.

Neither did the suspicions against him remain passive; they became active.

Goldsmiths' bills, to the amount of several thousand pounds, had been taken in the packet and Hiram was examined with an almost inquisitorial closeness and strictness as to whether he had or had not knowledge of their whereabouts.

Under his accumulated misfortunes, he grew not only more dull, more taciturn, than ever, but gloomy, moody, brooding as well. For hours he would sit staring straight before him into the fire, without moving so much as a hair.

One night—it was a bitterly cold night in February, with three inches of dry and gritty snow upon the ground—while Hiram sat thus brooding, there came, of a sudden, a soft tap upon the door.

Low and hesitating as it was, Hiram started violently at the sound. He sat for a while, looking from right to left. Then suddenly pushing back his chair, he arose, strode to the door, and flung it wide open.

It was Sally Martin.

Hiram stood for a while staring blankly at her. It was she who first spoke. "Won't you let me come in, Hi?" said she. "I'm nigh starved with the cold and I'm fit to die, I'm so hungry. For God's sake, let me come in."

"Yes," said Hiram, "I'll let you come in, but why don't you go home?"

The poor girl was shivering and chattering with the cold; now she began crying, wiping her eyes with the corner of a blanket in which her head and shoulders were wrapped. "I have been home, Hiram," she said, "but dad, he shut the door in my face. He cursed me just awful, Hi— I wish I was dead!"

"You better come in," said Hiram. "It's no good standing out there in the cold." He stood aside and the girl entered, swiftly, gratefully.

At Hiram's bidding black Dinah presently set some food before Sally and she fell to eating ravenously, almost ferociously. Meantime, while she ate, Hiram stood with his back to the fire, looking at her face that face once so round and rosy, now thin, pinched, haggard.

"Are you sick, Sally?" said he presently.

"No," said she, "but I've had pretty hard times since I left home, Hi." The tears sprang to her eyes at the recollection of her troubles, but she only wiped them hastily away with the back of her hand, without stopping in her eating.

A long pause of dead silence followed. Dinah sat crouched together on a cricket at the other side of the hearth, listening with interest. Hiram did not seem to see her. "Did you go off with Levi?" said he at last, speaking abruptly. The girl looked up furtively under her brows. "You needn't be afeared to tell," he added.

"Yes," said she at last, "I did go off with him, Hi."

"Where've you been?"

At the question, she suddenly laid down her knife and fork.

"Don't you ask me that, Hi," said she, agitatedly, "I can't tell you that. You don't know Levi, Hiram; I darsn't tell you anything he don't want me to. If I told you where I been he'd hunt me out, no matter where I was, and kill me. If you only knew what I know about him, Hiram, you wouldn't ask anything about him."

Hiram stood looking broodingly at her for a long time; then at last he again spoke. "I thought a sight of you onc't, Sally," said he.

Sally did not answer immediately, but, after a while, she suddenly looked up. "Hiram," said she, "if I tell ye something will you promise on your oath not to breathe a word to any living soul?" Hiram nodded. "Then I'll tell you, but if Levi finds I've told he'll murder me as sure as you're standin' there. Come nigher—I've got to whisper it." He leaned forward close to her where she sat. She looked swiftly from right to left; then raising her lips she breathed into his ear: "I'm an honest woman, Hi. I was married to Levi West before I run away."

The winter had passed, spring had passed, and summer had come. Whatever Hiram had felt, he had made no sign of suffering. Nevertheless, his lumpy face had begun to look flabby, his cheeks hollow, and his loose-jointed body shrunk more awkwardly together into its clothes. He was often awake at night, sometimes walking up and down his room until far into the small hours.

It was through such a wakeful spell as this that he entered into the greatest, the most terrible, happening of his life.

It was a sulphurously hot night in July. The air was like the breath of a furnace, and it was a hard matter to sleep with even the easiest mind and under the most favorable circumstances. The full moon shone in through the open window, laying a white square of light upon the floor, and Hiram, as he paced up and down, up and down, walked directly through it, his gaunt figure starting out at every turn into sudden brightness as he entered the straight line of misty light.

The clock in the kitchen whirred and rang out the hour of twelve, and Hiram stopped in his walk to count the strokes.

The last vibration died away into silence, and still he stood motionless, now listening with a new and sudden intentness, for, even as the clock rang the last stroke, he heard soft, heavy footsteps, moving slowly and cautiously along the pathway before the house and directly below the open window. A few seconds more and he heard the creaking of rusty hinges. The mysterious visitor had entered the mill. Hiram crept softly to the window and looked out. The moon shone full on the dusty, shingled face of the old mill, not thirty steps away, and he saw that the door was standing wide open. A second or two of stillness followed, and then, as he still stood looking intently, he saw the figure of a man suddenly appear, sharp and vivid, from the gaping blackness of the open doorway. Hiram could see his face as clear as day. It was Levi West, and he carried an empty meal bag over his arm.

Levi West stood looking from right to left for a second or two, and then he took off his hat and wiped his brow with the back of his hand. Then he softly closed the door behind him and left the mill as he had come, and with the same cautious step. Hiram looked down upon him as he passed close to the house and almost directly beneath. He could have touched him with his hand.

Fifty or sixty yards from the house Levi stopped and a second figure arose from the black shadow in the angle of the worm fence and joined him. They stood for a while talking together, Levi pointing now and then toward the mill. Then the two turned, and, climbing over the fence, cut across an open field and through the tall, shaggy grass toward the southeast.

Hiram straightened himself and drew a deep breath, and the moon, shining full upon his face, showed it twisted, convulsed, as it had been when he had fronted his stepbrother seven months before in the kitchen. Great beads of sweat stood on his brow and he wiped them away with his sleeve. Then, coatless, hatless as he was, he swung himself out of the window, dropped upon the grass, and, without an instant of hesitation, strode off down the road in the direction that Levi West had taken.

As he climbed the fence where the two men had climbed it he could see them in the pallid light, far away across the level, scrubby meadow land, walking toward a narrow strip of pine woods.

A little later they entered the sharp-cut shadows beneath the trees and were swallowed in the darkness.

With fixed eyes and close-shut lips, as doggedly, as inexorably as though he were a Nemesis hunting his enemy down, Hiram followed their footsteps across the stretch of moonlit open. Then, by and by, he also was in the shadow of the pines. Here, not a sound broke the midnight hush. His feet made no noise upon the resinous softness of the ground below. In that dead, pulseless silence he could distinctly hear the distant voices of Levi and his companion, sounding loud and resonant in the hollow of the woods. Beyond the woods was a cornfield, and presently he heard the rattling of the harsh leaves as the two plunged into the tasseled jungle. Here, as in the woods, he followed them, step by step, guided by the noise of their progress through the canes.

Beyond the cornfield ran a road that, skirting to the south of Lewes, led across a wooden bridge to the wide salt marshes that stretched between the town and the distant sand hills. Coming out upon this road Hiram found that he had gained upon those he followed, and that they now were not fifty paces away, and he could see that Levi's companion carried over his shoulder what looked like a bundle of tools.

He waited for a little while to let them gain their distance and for the second time wiped his forehead with his shirt sleeve; then, without ever once letting his eyes leave them, he climbed the fence to the roadway.

For a couple of miles or more he followed the two along the white, level highway, past silent, sleeping houses, past barns, sheds, and haystacks, looming big in the moonlight, past fields, and woods, and clearings, past the dark and silent skirts of the town, and so, at last, out upon the wide, misty salt marshes, which seemed to stretch away interminably through the pallid light, yet were bounded in the far distance by the long, white line of sand hills.

Across the level salt marshes he followed them, through the rank sedge and past the glassy pools in which his own inverted image stalked beneath as he stalked above; on and on, until at last they had reached a belt of scrub pines, gnarled and gray, that fringed the foot of the white sand hills.

Here Hiram kept within the black network of shadow. The two whom he followed walked more in the open, with their shadows, as black as ink, walking along in the sand beside them, and now, in the dead, breathless stillness, might be heard, dull and heavy, the distant thumping, pounding roar of the Atlantic surf, beating on the beach at the other side of the sand hills, half a mile away.

At last the two rounded the southern end of the white bluff, and when Hiram, following, rounded it also, they were no longer to be seen.

Before him the sand hill rose, smooth and steep, cutting in a sharp ridge against the sky. Up this steep hill trailed the footsteps of those he followed, disappearing over the crest. Beyond the ridge lay a round, bowllike hollow, perhaps fifty feet across and eighteen or twenty feet deep, scooped out by the eddying of the winds into an almost perfect circle. Hiram, slowly, cautiously, stealthily, following their trailing line of footmarks, mounted to the top of the hillock and peered down into the bowl beneath. The two men were sitting upon the sand, not far from the tall, skeleton-like shaft of a dead pine tree that rose, stark and gray, from the sand in which it may once have been buried, centuries ago.

Levi had taken off his coat and waistcoat and was fanning himself with his hat. He was sitting upon the bag he had brought from the mill and that he had spread out upon the sand. His companion sat facing him. The moon shone full upon him and Hiram knew him instantly—he was the same burly, foreign-looking ruffian who had come with the little man to the mill that night to see Levi. He also had his hat off and was wiping his forehead and face with a red handkerchief. Beside him lay the bundle of tools he had brought—a couple of shovels, a piece of rope, and a long, sharp iron rod.

The two men were talking together, but Hiram could not understand what they said, for they spoke in the same foreign language that they had before used. But he could see his stepbrother point with his finger, now to the dead tree and now to the steep, white face of the opposite side of the bowllike hollow.

At last, having apparently rested themselves, the conference, if conference it was, came to an end, and Levi led the way, the other following, to the dead pine tree. Here he stopped and began searching, as though for some mark; then, having found that which he looked for, he drew a tapeline and a large brass pocket compass from his pocket. He gave one end of the tape line to his companion, holding the other with his thumb pressed upon a particular part of the tree. Taking his bearings by the compass, he gave now and then some orders to the other, who moved a little to the left or the right as he bade. At last he gave a word of command, and, thereupon, his companion drew a wooden peg from his pocket and thrust it into the sand. From this peg as a base they again measured, taking bearings by the compass, and again drove a peg. For a third time they repeated their measurements and then, at last, seemed to have reached the point which they aimed for.

Here Levi marked a cross with his heel upon the sand.

His companion brought him the pointed iron rod that lay beside the shovels, and then stood watching as Levi thrust it deep into the sand, again and again, as though sounding for some object below. It was some while before he found that for which he was seeking, but at last the rod struck with a jar upon some hard object below. After making sure of success by one or two additional taps with the rod, Levi left it remaining where it stood, brushing the sand from his hands. "Now fetch the shovels, Pedro," said he, speaking for the first time in English.

The two men were busy for a long while, shoveling away the sand. The object for which they were seeking lay buried some six feet deep, and the work was heavy and laborious, the shifting sand sliding back, again and again, into the hole. But at last the blade of one of the shovels struck upon some hard substance and Levi stooped and brushed away the sand with the palm of his hand.

Levi's companion climbed out of the hole that they had dug and tossed the rope that he had brought with the shovels down to the other. Levi made it fast to some object below and then himself mounted to the level of the sand above. Pulling together, the two drew up from the hole a heavy iron-bound box, nearly three feet long and a foot wide and deep.

Levi's companion stooped and began untying the rope which had been lashed to a ring in the lid.

What next happened happened suddenly, swiftly, terribly. Levi drew back a single step, and shot one quick, keen look to right and to left. He passed his hand rapidly behind his back, and the next moment Hiram saw the moonlight gleam upon the long, sharp, keen blade of a knife. Levi raised his arm. Then, just as the other arose from bending over the chest, he struck, and struck again, two swift, powerful blows. Hiram saw the blade drive, clean and sharp, into the back, and heard the hilt strike with a dull thud against the ribs—once, twice. The burly, black-bearded wretch gave a shrill, terrible cry and fell staggering back. Then, in an instant, with another cry, he was up and clutched Levi with a clutch of despair by the throat and by the arm. Then followed a struggle, short, terrible, silent. Not a sound was heard but the deep, panting breath and the scuffling of feet in the sand, upon which there now poured and dabbled a dark-purple stream. But it was a one-sided struggle and lasted only for a second or two. Levi wrenched his arm loose from the wounded man's grasp, tearing his shirt sleeve from the wrist to the shoulder as he did so. Again and again the cruel knife was lifted, and again and again it fell, now no longer bright, but stained with red.

Then, suddenly, all was over. Levi's companion dropped to the sand without a sound, like a bundle of rags. For a moment he lay limp and inert; then one shuddering spasm passed over him and he lay silent and still, with his face half buried in the sand.

Levi, with the knife still gripped tight in his hand, stood leaning over his victim, looking down upon his body. His shirt and hand, and even his naked arm, were stained and blotched with blood. The moon lit up his face and it was the face of a devil from hell.

At last he gave himself a shake, stooped and wiped his knife and hand and arm upon the loose petticoat breeches of the dead man. He thrust his knife back into its sheath, drew a key from his pocket and unlocked the chest. In the moonlight Hiram could see that it was filled mostly with paper and leather bags, full, apparently of money.

All through this awful struggle and its awful ending Hiram lay, dumb and motionless, upon the crest of the sand hill, looking with a horrid fascination upon the death struggle in the pit below. Now Hiram arose. The sand slid whispering down from the crest as he did so, but Levi was too intent in turning over the contents of the chest to notice the slight sound.

Hiram's face was ghastly pale and drawn. For one moment he opened his lips as though to speak, but no word came. So, white, silent, he stood for a few seconds, rather like a statue than a living man, then, suddenly, his eyes fell upon the bag that Levi had brought with him, no doubt, to carry back the treasure for which he and his companion were in search, and that still lay spread out on the sand where it had been flung. Then, as though a thought had suddenly flashed upon him, his whole expression changed, his lips closed tightly together as though fearing an involuntary sound might escape, and the haggard look dissolved from his face.

Cautiously, slowly, he stepped over the edge of the sand hill and down the slanting face. His coming was as silent as death, for his feet made no noise as he sank ankle deep in the yielding surface. So, stealthily, step by step, he descended, reached the bag, lifted it silently. Levi, still bending over the chest and searching through the papers within, was not four feet away. Hiram raised the bag in his hands. He must have made some slight rustle as he did so, for suddenly Levi half turned his head. But he was one instant too late. In a flash the bag was over his head—shoulders—arms—body.

Then came another struggle, as fierce, as silent, as desperate as that other—and as short. Wiry, tough, and strong as he was, with a lean, sinewy, nervous vigor, fighting desperately for his life as he was, Levi had no chance against the ponderous strength of his stepbrother. In any case, the struggle could not have lasted long; as it was, Levi stumbled backward over the body of his dead mate and fell, with Hiram upon him. Maybe he was stunned by the fall; maybe he felt the hopelessness of resistance, for he lay quite still while Hiram, kneeling upon him, drew the rope from the ring of the chest and, without uttering a word, bound it tightly around both the bag and the captive within, knotting it again and again and drawing it tight. Only once was a word spoken. "If you'll lemme go," said a muffled voice from the bag, "I'll give you five thousand pounds—it's in that there box." Hiram answered never a word, but continued knotting the rope and drawing it tight.

The *Scorpion* sloop-of-war lay in Lewes harbor all that winter and spring, probably upon the slim chance of a return of the pirates. It was about eight o'clock in the morning and Lieutenant Maynard was sitting in Squire Hall's office, fanning himself with his hat and talking in a desultory fashion. Suddenly the dim and distant noise of a great crowd was heard from without, coming nearer and nearer. The Squire and his visitor hurried to the door. The crowd was coming down the street shouting, jostling, struggling, some on the footway, some in the roadway. Heads were at the doors and windows, looking down upon them. Nearer they came, and nearer; then at last they could see that the press surrounded and accompanied one man. It was Hiram White, hatless, coatless, the sweat running down his face in streams, but stolid and silent as ever. Over his shoulder he carried a bag, tied round and round with a rope. It was not until the crowd and the man it surrounded had come quite near that the Squire and the lieutenant saw that a pair of legs in gray-yarn stockings hung from the bag. It was a man he was carrying.

Hiram had lugged his burden five miles that morning without help and with scarcely a rest on the way.

He came directly toward the Squire's office and, still sun rounded and hustled by the crowd, up the steep steps to the office within. He flung his burden heavily upon the floor without a word and wiped his streaming forehead.

The Squire stood with his knuckles on his desk, staring first at Hiram and then at the strange burden he had brought. A sudden hush fell upon all, though the voices of those without sounded as loud and turbulent as ever. "What is it, Hiram?" said Squire Hall at last.

Then for the first time Hiram spoke, panting thickly. "It's a bloody murderer," said he, pointing a quivering finger at the motionless figure.

"Here, some of you!" called out the Squire. "Come! Untie this man! Who is he?" A dozen willing fingers quickly unknotted the rope and the bag was slipped from the head and body.

Hair and face and eyebrows and clothes were powdered with meal, but, in spite of all and through all the innocent whiteness, dark spots and blotches and smears of blood showed upon head and arm and shirt. Levi raised himself upon his elbow and looked scowlingly around at the amazed, wonderstruck faces surrounding him.

"Why, it's Levi West!" croaked the Squire, at last finding his voice.

Then, suddenly, Lieutenant Maynard pushed forward, before the others crowded around the figure on the floor, and, clutching Levi by the hair, dragged his head backward so as to better see his face. "Levi West!" said he in a loud voice. "Is this the Levi West you've been telling me of? Look at that scar and the mark on his cheek! THIS IS BLUE-SKIN HIMSELF."

In the chest that Blueskin had dug up out of the sand were found not only the goldsmiths' bills taken from the packet, but also many other valuables belonging to the officers and the passengers of the unfortunate ship.

The New York agents offered Hiram a handsome reward for his efforts in recovering the lost bills, but Hiram declined it, positively and finally. "All I want," said he, in his usual dull, stolid fashion, "is to have folks know I'm honest." Nevertheless, though he did not accept what the agents of the packet offered, fate took the matter into its own hands and rewarded him not unsubstantially. Blueskin was taken to England in the *Scorpion*. But he never came to trial. While in Newgate he hanged himself to the cell window with his own stockings. The news of his end was brought to Lewes in the early autumn and Squire Hall took immediate measures to have the five hundred pounds of his father's legacy duly transferred to Hiram.

In November Hiram married the pirate's widow.

The Life of Captain Lowther

BY CAPTAIN CHARLES JOHNSON

George Lowther sailed out of the river of Thames, in one of the Royal African Company's ships, called the *Gambia Castle*, of 16 guns and thirty men, Charles Russel commander; of which ship, the said Lowther was second mate. Aboard of the same ship, was a certain number of soldiers, commanded by one John Massey who were to be carried to one of the Company's settlements, on the river of Gambia, to garrison a fort, which was sometime ago taken and destroyed, by Captain Davis the pirate.

In May 1721, the *Gambia Castle* came safe to her port in Africa, and landed Captain Massey and his men on James's Island, where he was to command under the governor, Colonel Whitney, who arrived there at the same time, in another ship. And here, by a fatal misunderstanding, between the military folks and the trading people, the fort and garrison not only came to be lost again to the Company, but a fine galley well provided, and worth 10,000 pounds turned against her masters.

The names of the governor and captain sounded great, but when the gentlemen found that the power that generally goes along with those titles was overswayed and born down by the merchants and factors (mechanic fellows as they thought them), they grew very impatient and disatisfied, especially Massey, who was very loud in his complaints against them, particularly at the small allowance of provisions to him and his men; for the garrison and governor too, were victualled by the merchants, which was no small grievance and mortification to them. And as the want of eating was the only thing that made the great Sancho quit his government, so did it here rend and tear their's to pieces. For Massey told them, that he did not come here to be a Guinea slave, and that he had promised his men good treatment, and provisions fitting for soldiers: that if he had the care of so many of His Majesty's subjects, if they would not provide for them in a handsome manner, he should take suitable measures for the preservation of so many of his countrymen and companions.

The governor at this time was very ill of a fever, and, for the better accommodation in his sickness, was carried aboard the ship *Gambia Castle*, where he continued for about three weeks, and therefore could have little to say in this dispute, though he resolved not to stay in a place where there was so little occasion for him, and where his power was so confined. The merchants had certainly orders from the Company, to issue the provisions out to the garrison, and the same is done along the whole coast; but whether they had cut them short of the allowance that was appointed them, I can't say, but if they did, then is the loss of the ship and garrison owing principally to their ill conduct.

However, an accident that happened on board the ship did not a little contribute to this misfortune, which was a pique that the captain of her took against his second mate, George Lowther, the man who is the subject of this short history; and who losing his favor, found means to ingratiate himself into the good liking of the common sailors, insomuch that when Captain Russel ordered him to be punished, the men took up handspikes, and threatened to knock that man down that offered to lay hold of the mate. This served but to widen the differences between him and the captain, and more firmly attached Lowther to the ship's company, the greatest part of which, he found ripe for any mischief in the world.

Captain Massey was no wit the better reconciled to the place, by a longer continuance, nor to the usage he met with there, and having often opportunities of conversing with Lowther, with whom he had contracted an intimacy in the voyage, they aggravated one another's grievances to such a height, that they resolved upon measures to curb the power that controlled them, and to provide for themselves after another manner.

When the governor recovered of his fever, he went ashore to the island, but took no notice of Massey's behavior, though it was such as might give suspicion of what he designed; and Lowther, and the common sailors, who were in the secret of affairs, grew insolent and bold, even refusing to obey when commanded to their duty by Captain Russel and the chief mate. The captain seeing how things were carried goes ashore early one morning to the governor and factory, in order to hold a council, which Lowther apprehending was in order to prevent his design, sent a letter in the same boat to Massey, intimating it to him, and that he should repair on board, for it was high time to put their project in execution.

As soon as Massey received this letter, he went to the soldiers at the barracks, and said to them, and others, "You that have a mind to go to England, now is our time"; and they generally consenting, Massey went to the storeroom, burst open the door, set two sentinels upon it, and ordered that nobody should come near it; then he went to the governor's apartment, and took his bed, baggage, plate, and furniture (in expectation that the governor himself, as he had promised Massey, would have gone on board, which he afterwards refused, by reason, as he said, he believed they were going a-pirating; which at first, whatever Lowther designed, Massey certainly proposed only the going to England); when this was done, he sent the boat off to the chief mate, with this message, that he should get the guns ready, for that the King of Barro [a Negro kingdom near the Royal African settlement] would come aboard to dinner. But Lowther understanding best the meaning of those orders, he confined the chief mate, shotted the guns, and put the ship in a condition for sailing. In the afternoon Massey came on board with the governor's son, having sent off all the provisions of the island, and eleven pipes of wines, leaving only two half pipes behind the storehouse, and dismounted all the guns of the fort.

In the afternoon they weighed one anchor, but fearing to be too late to get out of the river, they slipped the other, and so fell down; in doing of which, they run the ship aground. Massey showed himself a soldier upon this accident, for as soon as the misfortune happened, he left the ship with about sixteen hands, and rows directly to the fort, remounts the guns, and keeps garrison there all the night, while the ship was ashore; and obliged some of the factory to assist in getting her clear. In the meanwhile, Russel came off, but not being suffered to come on board, he called to Lowther, and offered him and the company, whatever terms they would be pleased to accept of, upon condition of surrendering up the ship, which had no effect upon any of them. In the morning they got her afloat, and Massey and his men came aboard, after having nailed up and dismounted all the cannon of the fort. They put the governor's son, and two or three others ashore, who were not willing to go without the governor, and sailed out of the river, having exchanged several shot with the *Martha, Otter,* etc. that lay there, without doing execution on either side.

When the ship came out to sea, Lowther called up all the company, and told them it was the greatest folly imaginable, to think of returning to England, for what they had already done, could not be justified upon any pretence whatsoever, but would be looked upon, in the eye of the law, a capital offence, and that none of them were in a condition to withstand the attacks of such powerful adversaries, as they would meet with at home; for his part he was determined not to run such a hazard, and therefore if his proposal was not agreed to, he desired to be set ashore in some place of safety; that they had a good ship under them, a parcel of brave fellows in her, that it was not their business to starve, or be made slaves; and therefore, if they were all of his mind, they should seek their fortunes upon the seas, as other adventurers had done before them. They one and all came into the measures, knocked down the cabins, made the ship flush for and aft, prepared black colors, new named her, the *Delivery*, having about fifty hands and 16 guns, and the following short articles were drawn up, signed and sworn to upon the bible.

The Articles of Captain Ggeorge Lowther, & His Company

1. The Captain is to have two full Shares; the Master is to have one Share and a half; The Doctor, Mate, Gunner & Boatswain, one Share and a quarter.

2. He that shall be found Guilty of taking up any unlawful Weapon on Board the Privateer, or any Prize, by us taken, so as to strike or abuse one another, in any regard, shall suffer what Punishment the Captain and Majority of the Company shall think fit.

3. He that shall be found Guilty of Cowardize, in the Time of Engagement, shall suffer what Punishment the Captain and Majority shall think fit.

4. If any Gold, Jewels, Silver, &c. be found on Board of any Prize or Prizes, to the value of a Piece of Eight; & the Finder do not deliver it to the Quarter-Master, in the Space of 24 Hours, shall suffer what Punishment the Captain and Majority shall think fit.

5. He that is found Guilty of Gaming, or Defrauding another to the Value of a Shilling, shall think fit.

6. He that shall have the Misfortune to lose a Limb, in time of Engagement, shall have the sum of one hundred and fifty Pounds Sterling, and remain with the Company as long as he shall think fit.

7. Good Quarters be given when called for.

8. He that sees Sail first, shall have the best Pistol, or Small-Arm, on Board her.

It was the 13th of June that Lowther left the settlement, and on the 20th, being then within 20 leagues of Barbados, he came up with a brigantine, belonging to Boston, called the *Charles*, James Douglass master, which they plundered in a piratical manner, and let the vessel go; but least he should meet with any of the station ships, and so give information of the robbery, *in terrorem*, to prevent a pursuit, Lowther contrived a sort of certificate, which he directed the master to show to their consort, and upon sight of it the brigantine would pass unmolested. This consort, he pretended, was a 40-gun ship, and cruising thereabouts.

After this the *Delivery* proceeded to Hispaniola; near the west end of the island she met with a French sloop laden with wine and brandy; aboard of this vessel went Captain Massey, as a merchant, and asked the price of one thing, and then another, bidding money for the greatest part of the cargo; then after he had trifled a while, he whispered a secret in the French man's ear, viz., that they must have it all without money, Monsieur presently understanding his meaning, and unwillingly agreed to the bargain. They took out of her thirty casks of brandy, five hogsheads of wine, several pieces of chintzes, and other valuable goods, and seventy pounds English, in money; of which Lowther generously returned five pounds back to the French master for his civilities.

But as all constitutions grow old, and thereby shake and totter, so did our commonwealth in about a month of its age, feel commotions and intestine disturbances, by the divisions of its member, which had near hand terminated in its destruction; these civil discords were owing to the following occasion. Captain Massey had been a solider almost from his infancy, but was but very indifferently acquainted with maritime affairs, and having an enterprizing soul, nothing would satisfy him, but he must be doing business in his own way, therefore he required Lowther to let him have thirty hands to land with, and he would attack the French settlements, and bring aboard the devil and all the plunder.

Lowther did all that he could, and said all that he could say, to dissuade Massey from so rash and dangerous an attempt; pointing out to him the hazard the company would run, and the consequences to them all, if he should not succeed, and the little likelihood there was to expect success from the undertaking. But 'twas all one for that, Massey would go and attack the French settlements, for anything Lowther could say against it; so that he was obliged to propose the matter to the company, among whom Massey found a few fellows as resolute as himself; however, a great majority being against it, the affair was overruled in opposition to Captain Massey, notwithstanding which, Massey grew fractious, quarrelled with Lowther, and the men divided into parties, some siding with the land pirate, and some with the sea rover, and were all ready to fall together by the ears, when the man at the masthead cried out, "A sail! A sail!" Then they gave over the dispute, set all their sails, and steered after the chase. In a few hours they came up with her, she being a small ship from Jamaica, bound to England; they took what they thought fit out of her, and a hand or two, and then Lowther was for sinking the ship, with several passengers that were in her, for what reason I know not, but Massey so that he interposed, prevented their cruel fate, and the ship safely arrived afterwards in England.

The next day they took a small sloop, an interloping trader, which they detained with her cargo. All this while Massey was uneasy, and declared his resolution to leave them, and Lowther finding him a very troublesome man to deal with, consented that he should take the sloop, last made prize of, with what hands had a mind to go with him, and shift for himself. Whereupon Massey, with about ten more malcontents, goes aboard the sloop, and comes away in her directly for Jamaica.

Notwithstanding what had passed, Captain Massey puts a bold face upon the matter, and goes to Sir Nicholas Laws, the governor, informs him of his leaving Lowther the pirate, owns that he assisted in going off with the ship, at the River Gambia; but said, 'twas to save so many of His Majesty's subjects from perishing, and that his design was to return to England; but Lowther conspiring with the great part of the company, went a-pirating with the ship; and that he had taken this opportunity to leave him, and surrender himself and vessel to his excellency.

Massey was very well received by the governor, and had his liberty given him, with a promise of his favor, and so forth; and at his own request, he was sent on board the *Happy* sloop, Captain Laws, to cruise off Hispaniola, for Lowther; but not being so fortunate as to meet with him, Captain Massey returned back to Jamaica in the sloop, and getting a certificate, and a supply of money, from the governor, he came home passenger to England.

When Massey came to town, he writes a long letter to the deputy governor and directors of the African Company, wherein he imprudently relates the whole transactions of his voyage, the going off with the ship, and the acts of piracy he had committed with Lowther; but excuses it as rashness and inadvertency in himself, occasioned by his being ill used, contrary to the promises that had been made him, and the expectations he had entertained; but owned, that he deserved to die for what he had done; yet, if they had generosity enough to forgive him, as he was still capable to do them service, as a soldier, so he should be very ready to do it; but if they resolved to prosecute him, he begged only this favor, that he might not be hanged like a dog but to die like a soldier, as he had been bred from his childhood, that is, that he might be shot.

This was the substance of the letter, which, however, did not produce so favorable an answer as he hoped for, word being brought back to him, that he should be fairly hanged. Whereupon, Massey resolved not be out of the way, when he found what important occasion there was likely to be for him, but takes a lodging in Aldersgate Street, the next day went to the Lord Chief Justice's chambers, and enquired, if my lord had granted a warrant against Captain John Massey, for piracy. But being told by the clerks, that they knew of no such thing, he informed them, he was the man that my lord would soon be applied to for that purpose, and the officer might come to him at such a place, where he lodged. They took the directions in writing, and, in a few days, a warrant being issued, the tipstaff went directly, by his own information, and apprehended him, without any other trouble, than walking to his lodging.

There was then no person in town to charge him with any fact, upon which he could be committed; nor could the letter be proved to be of his handwriting, so that they had been obliged to let him go again, if he had not helped his accusers out a pinch. The magistrate was reduced to putting of this question to him, "Did you write this letter?" He answered, he did. And not only that, but confessed all the contents of it; upon which, he was committed to Newgate, but was afterwards admitted to 100 pounds bail, or thereabouts.

On the 5th July 1723, he was brought to his trial, at a court of admiralty held at the Old Bailey, when Captain Russel, Governor Whitney's son, and others, appeared as evidences, by whom the indictment was plainly proved against him; which, if it had not been done, the captain was of such an heroic spirit that he would have denied nothing; for instead of making a defense, he only entertained the court with a long narrative of his expedition, from the first setting out, to his return to England, mentioning two acts of piracy committed by him, which he was not charged with, often challenging the evidences of contradict him, if in anything he related the least syllable of an untruth; and instead of denying the crimes set forth in the indictment, he charged himself with various circumstances, which fixed the facts more home upon him. Upon the whole, the captain was found guilty, received sentence of death, and was executed three weeks after, at Execution Dock.

We return now to Lowther, whom we left cruising off Hispaniola, from whence he plied to windward, and near Puerto Rico, chased two sail, and spoke with them; they proving to be a small Bristol ship, commanded by Captain Smith, and a Spanish pirate, who had made prize of the said ship. Lowther examined into the Spaniard's authority for taking an English vessel, and threatened to put every man of them to death, for so doing; so that the Spaniards fancied themselves to be in a very pitiful condition, till matters cleared up, and they found their masters as great rogues as themselves, from whom some mercy might be expected, in regard to the near relation they stood with them, as to their profession; in short, Lowther first rifled, and then burnt both the ships, sending the Spaniards away in their launch, and turning all the English sailors into pirates.

After a few days cruise, Lowther took a small sloop belonging to St. Christophers, which they manned and carried along with them to a small island, where they cleaned, and stayed some time to take their diversions, which consisted in unheard of debaucheries, with drinking, swearing and rioting, in which there seemed to be a kind of emulation

among them, resembling rather devils than men, striving who should outdo one another in new invented oaths and execrations.

They all got aboard about Christmas, observing neither times nor seasons, for perpetrating their villainous actions, and sailed towards the Bay of Honduras; but stopping at the Grand Caymans for water, they met with a small vessel with thirteen hands, in the same honorable employment with themselves; the captain of this gang was one Edward Low, whom we shall particularly discourse of in a chapter by itself. Lowther received them as friends, and treated them with all imaginable respect, inviting them, as they were few in number, and in no condition to pursue the account (as they called it), to join their strength together, which on the consideration aforesaid, was accepted of, Lowther still continuing commander, and Lowe was made lieutenant. The vessel the new pirates come out of, they sunk, and the confederates proceed on the voyage as Lowther before intended.

The 10th of January, the pirates came into the bay, and fell upon a ship of 200 tons, called the *Greyhound*, Benjamin Edwards commander, belonging to Boston. Lowther hoisted his piratical colors, and fired a gun for the *Greyhound* to bring to, which she refusing, the *Happy Delivery* (the name of the pirate) edged down, and gave her a broadside, which was returned by Captain Edwards very bravely, and the engagement held for an hour; but Captain Edwards, finding the pirate too strong for him, and fearing the consequence of too obstinate a resistance, against those lawless fellows, ordered his ensign to be struck. The pirates boat came aboard, and not only rifled the ship, but whipped, beat, and cut the men in a cruel manner, turned them aboard their own ship, and then set fire to theirs.

In cruising about the bay, they met and took several other vessels without any resistance, viz., two brigantines of Boston in New England, one of which they burnt, and sunk the other; a sloop belonging to Conneticut, Captain Airs, which they also burnt; a sloop of Jamaica, Captain Hamilton, they took for their own use; a sloop of Virginia they unladed, and was so generous as to give her back to the master that owned her. They took a sloop of 100 tons, belonging to Rhode Island, which they were pleased to keep, and mount with 8 carriage, and 10 swivel guns.

With this little fleet, viz., Admiral Lowther, in the *Happy Delivery*; Captain Low, in the Rhode Island sloop; Captain Harris (who was second mate in the *Greyhound* when taken), in Hamilton's sloop; and the little sloop formerly mentioned, serving as a tender; I say, with this fleet, the pirates left the bay, and came to Port Mayo in the Gulf of Matique, and there made preparations to careen; they carried ashore all their sails, and made tents by the waterside, wherein they laid their plunder, stores, etc. and fell to work; and at the time when the ships were upon the heel, and the good folks employed in heaving down, scrubbing, tallowing, and so forth; of a sudden came down a considerable body of the natives, and attacked the pirates unprepared. As they were in no condition to defend themselves, they fled to their sloops, leaving them masters of the field and the spoil thereof, which was of great value, and set fire to the *Happy Delivery*, their capital ship.

Lowther made the best provision he could in the largest sloop, which he called the *Ranger*, having 10 guns and 8 swivels, and she sailing best, the company went all aboard of her, and left the other at sea. Provisions was now very short, which, with the late loss, put them in a confounded ill humor, insomuch that they were every now and then, going together by the ears, laying the blame of their ill conduct sometimes upon one, then upon another.

The beginning of May 1722, they got to the West Indies, and near the island of Diseada, took a brigantine, one Payne master, that afforded them what they stood in need of, which put them in better temper, and business seemed to go well again. After they had pretty well plundered the brigantine, they sent her to the bottom. They went into the island and watered, and then stood to the northward, intending to visit the main coast of America.

In the latitude of 38°, they took a brigantine called the *Rebecca* of Boston, Captain Smith, bound thither from St. Christophers. At the taking of this vessel, the crews divided; for Low, whom Lowther joined at the Grand Caymans, proving always a very unruly member of the commonwealth, always aspiring, and never satisfied with the proceedings of the commander; he thought it the safest way to get rid of him, upon any terms; and according to the vote of the company, they parted the bear skin between them: Low with forty-four hands went aboard the brigantine, and Lowther with the same number stayed in the sloop, and separated that very night, being the 28th of May 1722.

Lowther proceeding on his way to the main coast, took three or four fishing vessels off New York, which was no great booty to the captors. The 3rd of June, they met with a small New England ship, bound home from Barbados, which stood an attack a small time, but finding it to no purpose, yielded herself a prey to the booters. The pirates took out of her fourteen hogsheads of rum, six barrels of sugar, a large box of English goods, several casks of loaf sugar, a considerable quantity of pepper, six Negroes, besides a sum of money and plate, and then let her go on her voyage.

The next adventure was not so fortunate for them, for coming pretty near the coast of South Carolina, they met with a ship just come out, on her voyage to England; Lowther gave her a gun, and hoisted his piratical colors; but this ship, which was called the *Amy*, happening to have a brave gallant man to command her, who was not any ways daunted with that terrible ensign, the black flag, he instead of striking immediately, as 'twas expected, let fly a broadside at the pirate. Lowther (not at all pleased with the compliment, though he put up with it for the present) was for taking leave; but the *Amy* getting the pirate between her and the shore, stood after him to clap him aboard; to prevent which, Lowther run the sloop aground, and landed all the men with their arms. Captain Gwatkins, the captain of the *Amy*, was obliged to stand off, for fear of running his own ship ashore; but at the same time thought fit for the public good, to destroy the enemy; and thereupon went into the boat, and rowed towards the sloop, in order to set her on fire; but before he reached the vessel, a fatal shot form Lowther's company ashore, put an end to their design and Captain Gwatkin's life. After this unfortunate blow, the mate returned aboard with the boat, and not being inclined to pursue them any farther, took charge of the ship.

Lowther got off the sloop after the departure of the *Amy*, and brought all his men aboard again, but was in a poor shattered condition, having suffered much in the engagement, and had a great many men killed and wounded. He made shift to get into an inlet somewhere in North Carolina, where he stayed a long while, before he was able to put to sea again.

He and his crew laid up all the winter, and shifted as well as they could among the woods, divided themselves into small parties, and hunted generally in the daytimes. Killing of black cattle, hogs, etc. for their subsistence, and in the night retired to their tents and huts, which they made for lodging; and sometimes when the weather grew very cold, they would stay aboard of their sloop.

In the spring of the year 1723, they made shift to get to sea, and steered their course for Newfoundland, and upon the banks took a schooner, called the *Swift*, John Hood master; they found a good quantity of provisions aboard her, which they very much wanted at that time, and after taking three of their hands, and plundering her of what they thought fit, they let her depart. They took several other vessels upon the banks, and in the harbor, but none of any great account; and then steering for a warmer climate, in August at the West Indies. In their passage thither, they met with a brigantine, called the *John and Elizabeth*, Richard Stanny master, bound for Boston, which they plundered, took two of her men, and discharged her.

Lowther cruized a pretty while among the islands without any extraordinary success, and was reduced to a very small allowance of provisions, till they had the luck to fall in with a Martinique man-of-war, which proved a seasonable relief to them; and after that, a Guineaman had the ill fortune to become a prey to the rovers; she was called the *Princess*, Captain Wicksted commander.

It was now thought necessary to look out for a place to clean their sloop in, and prepare for new adventures. Accordingly the island of Blanco was pitched upon for that purpose, which lies in the latitude of 11° 50' north about thirty leagues from the main of the Spanish America, between the islands of Margarita and Rocas, and not far from Tortuga. It is a low even island, but healthy and dry, uninhabited, and about two leagues in circumference, with plenty of *lignum vitae* trees thereon, growing in spots, with shrubby bushes of other wood about them. There are, besides turtle, great numbers of guanoes, which is an amphibious creature like a lizard, but much larger, the body of it being as big as a man's leg; they are very good to eat, and are much used by the pirates that come here. They are of diverse colors, but such as live upon dry ground, as here at Blanco, are commonly yellow. On the northwest end of this island, there is a small cove or sandy bay, all round the rest of the island is deep water, and steep close to the island. Here Lowther resorted to, the beginning of October last, unrigged his sloop, sent his guns, sails, rigging, etc. ashore, and put his vessel upon the careen. The *Eagle* sloop of Barbados, belonging to the South Sea Company, with thirty-five hands, commanded by Walter Moore, coming near this island, in her voyage to Comena, on the Spanish continent, saw the said sloop just careened, with her guns out, and sails unbent, which she supposed to be a pirate, because it was a place where traders did not commonly use, so took the advantage of attacking her, as she was then unprepared; the *Eagle* having fired a gun to oblige her to show her colors, the pirate hoisted the St. George's flag at their topmast head, as it were to bid defiance to her; but when they found Moore and his crew resolved to board them in good earnest, the pirates cut their cable, and hauled their stern on shore, which obliged the *Eagle* to come to an anchor athwart their hawse, where she engaged them till they called for quarter and struck; at which time Lowther and twelve of the crew made their escape out of the cabin window. The master of the *Eagle* got the pirate sloop off, secured her, and went ashore with twenty-five hands, in pursuit of Lowther and his gang; but after five days search, they could find but five of them, which they brought aboard, and the proceeded with the sloop and pirates to Comena aforesaid, where they soon arrived.

The Spanish governor being informed of this brave action, condemned the sloop to the captors, and sent a small sloop with twenty-three hands to scour the bushes and other places of the island of Blanco, for the pirates that remained there, and took four more, with seven small arms, leaving behind them Captain Lowther, three men, and a little boy, which they could not take; the above four the Spaniards tried and condemned to slavery for life; three to the galleys, and the other to the Castle of Arraria.

The *Eagle* sloop brought all their prisoners afterwards to St. Christopher's, where the following were tried by a court of vice admiralty, there held March the 11th, 1722, viz., John Churchill, Edward Mackdonald, Nicolas Lewis, Richard West, Sam. Levercott, Robert White, John Shaw, Andrew Hunter, Jonathan Delve, Matthew Freebarn, Henry Watson, Roger Grange, Ralph Candor, and Robert Willis; the three last were acquitted, the other thirteen were found guilty, two of which were recommended to mercy by the court, and accordingly pardoned; and the rest executed at that island, on the 20th of the same month.

As for Captain Lowther, it is said that he afterwards shot himself upon that fatal island, where his piracies ended, being found, by some sloop's men, dead, and a pistol burst by his side.

chapter 9

The Life of Captain Anstis

BY CAPTAIN CHARLES JOHNSON

Thomas Anstis shipped himself at Providence in the year 1718, aboard the *Buck* sloop, and was one of six that conspired together to go off a-pirating with the vessel; the rest were, Howel Davis, Roberts's predecessor, killed at the island of Princes; Dennis Topping, killed at the taking of the rich Portugueze ship on the Coast of Brazil; Walter Kennedy, hanged at Execution Dok, and two other, which I forbear to name, because, I understand they are at this day employed in an honest vocation in the city.

What followed concerning Anstis's piracies has been included in the two preceding chapters; I shall only observe that the combination of these six men abovementioned, was the beginning of that company, that afterwards proved so formidable under Captain Roberts, from whom Anstis separated the 18th of April 1721, in the *Good Fortune* brigantine, leaving his commodore to pursue his adventures upon the coast of Guinea, whilst he returned to the West Indies, upon the like design.

About the middle of June, these pirates met with one Captain Marston, between Hispaniola and Jamaica, bound on a voyage to New

York, from whom they took all the wearing apparel they could find, as also his liquors and provision, and five of his men, but did not touch his cargo; two or three other vessels were also plundered by them, in this cruise, out of whom they stocked themselves with provision and men; among the rest, I think, was the *Irwin*, were in a condition to undertake something bold. But their government was disturbed by malecontents, and a kingdom divided within itself cannot stand. They had such a number of new men amongst them, that seemed not so violently inclined for the game; that whatever the captain proposed, 'twas certainly carried against him, so that they came to no fixed resolution for the undertaking any enterprize; therefore there was nothing to be done, but to break up the company, which seemed to be the inclination of the majority, but the manner of doing so, concerned their common safety; to which purpose various means were proposed, at length it was concluded to send home a petition to His Majesty (there being then no act of indemnity in force) for a pardon, and wait the issue; at the same time one Bones, boatswain of the *Good Fortune*, proposed a place of safe retreat, it being an uninhabited island near Cuba, which he had been used to in the late war, when he went a-privateering against the Spaniards.

This being approved of it was unanimously resolved on, and the underwritten petition drawn up and signed by the whole company in the manner of what they call a round-robin, that is, the names were written in a circle, to avoid all appearance of preeminence, and lest any person should be marked out by the government, as a principal rogue among them.

to his most sacred majesty george, by the grace of god, of great-britain, france and ireland, king, defender of the faith, &c.

The humble petition of the Company, now belonging to the Ship *Morning Star*, and Brigantine *Good Fortune*, lying under the ignominious Name and Denomination of pirates.

Humbly sheweth,

That we your Majesty's most loyal Subjects, have, at sundry Times, been taken by Bartholomew Roberts, the then Captain of the abovesaid Vessels and Company, together with another Ship, in which we left him; & have been forced by him & his Wicked Accomplices, to enter into, and serve, in the said Company, as Pyrates, much contrary to our Wills & Inclinations: And we your loyal Subjects utterly abhorring & detesting that impious way of living, did, with an unanimous Consent, and contrary to the knowledge of the said Roberts, or his Accomplices, on, or about the 18th May of April 1721, leave, & ran away with the aforesaid Ship *Morning Star,* & Brigantine *Good Fortune,* with no other Intent and Meaning than the Hopes of obtaining your Majesty's most gracious Pardon. And, that we your Majesty's most loyal Subjects, may with more safety return to our native Country, and serve the Nation, unto which we belong, in our respective Capacities, without Fear of being prosecuted by the Injured, whose Estates have suffered by the said Roberts and his Accomplices, during our forcible Detainment, by the said Company: we most humbly implore your Majesty's most royal Assent, to this our humble Petition.

And your Petitioners shall every Pray.

This petition was sent home by a merchant ship bound to England, from Jamaica, who promised to speak with the petitioners, in their return, about twenty leagues to windward of that island, and let them know what success their petition met with. When this was done, the pirates retired to the island before proposed, with the ship and brigantine.

The island (which I have no name for) lies off the southwest end of Cuba, uninhabited, and little frequented. On the east end is a lagoon, so narrow, that a ship can but just go in, though there's from fifteen-to twenty-two-foot water, for almost a league up. On both sides of the lagoon grow man mangrove trees, very thick, that the entrance of it, as well as the vessels laying there, is hardly to be seen. In the middle of the island are here and there a small thick wood of tall pines, and other trees scattered about in different places.

Here they stayed about nine months, but not having provision for above two, they were forced to take what the island afforded, which was fish of several sorts, particularly turtle, which latter was the chiefest food they lived on, and was found in great plenty on the coasts of this island; whether there might by any wild hogs, beef, or other cattle, common to several islands of the West Indies, or that the pirates were too idle to hunt them, or whether they preferred other provisions to that sort of diet, I know not; but I was informed by them, that for the whole time they eat not a bit of any kind of flesh-meat, nor bread; the latter was supplied by rice, of which they had a great quantity aboard: This they boiled and squeezed dry, and so ate with the turtle.

There are three or four sorts of these creatures in the West Indies, the largest of which will weigh 150 or 200 pounds weight or more, but those that were found upon this island were of the smallest kind, weighing 10 or 12 pounds each, with a fine natural wrought shell, and beautifully clouded; the meat sweet and tender, some part of it eating like chicken, some like veal, and so that it was no extraordinary hardship for them to live upon this provision alone, since it affords variety of meats to the taste, of itself. The manner of catching this fish is very particular; you must understand, that in the months of May, June and July, they lay their eggs in order to hatch their young, and this three times in a season, which is always in the sand of the seashore, each laying eighty or ninety eggs at a time. The male accompanies the female, and comes ashore in the night only, when they must be watched, without making any noise, or having a light; as soon as they land, the men that watch for them, turn them on their backs, then haul them above high-water mark, and leave them till next morning, where they are sure to find them, for they can't turn again, nor move from the place. It is to be observed, that besides their laying time, they come ashore to feed, but then what's very remarkable in this creatures, they always resort to different places to breed, leaving their usual haunts for two or three months, and 'tis thought they eat nothing in all that season.

They passed their time here in dancing, and other diversions agreeable to these sort of folks; and among the rest they appointed a mock court of judicature to try one another for piracy, and he that was a criminal one day was made judge another. I had an account given me of one of these merry trials, and as it appeared diverting, I shall give the readers a short acount of it.

The court and criminals being both appointed, as also council to plead, the judge got up in a tree, and had a dirty tarpaulin hung over his shoulders; this was done by way of robe, with a thrum cap on his head, and a large pair of spectacles upon his nose. Thus equipped, he settled himself in his place, and abundance of officers attending him below, with crows, handspikes, etc. instead of wands, tipstaves, and such like. The criminals were brought out, making a thousand sour faces; and one who acted as attorney general opened the charge against them; their speeches were very laconic, and their whole proceedings concise. We shall give it by way of dialogue.

Attorn. Gen: An't please your Lordship, and you Gentlemen of the Jury, here is a Fellow before you that is a sad Dog, a sad sad Dog; & I humbly hope your Lordship will order him to be hanged out of the Way immediately. He has committed Pyracy upon the High Seas, and we shall prove, an't please your Lordship, that his Fellow, this sad Dog before you, has escaped a thousand Storms, nay, has got safe ashore when the Ship has been cast away, which was a certain Sign he was not born to be drown'd; yet not having the Fear of hanging before his Eyes, he went on robbing & ravishing, Man, Woman and Child, plundering Ships Cargoes fore & aft, burning & sinking Ship, Bark and Boat, as if the Devil had been in him. But this is not all, my Lord, he has committed worse Villanies than all these, for we shall prove, that he has been guilty of drinking Small-Beer; and your Lordship knows, there never was a sober Fellow but what was a Rogue. My Lord, I should have spoke much finer than I do now, but that, as your Lordship knows our Rum is all out, and how should a Man speak good Law that has not drank a Dram. However, I hope, your Lordship will order the Follow to be hang'd.

Judge: Heark'ee me, sirrah, you lousy, pittiful, ill-look'd Dog; what have you to say why you should not be tuck'd up immediately, & set a Sundrying like a Scare-crow? Are you guilty, or not guilty?

Pris: Not guilty, an't please your Worship.

Judge: Not guilty! say so again, sirrah, and I'll have you hang'd without any Tryal.

Pris: An't please your Worship's Honour, my Lord, I am as honest a poor fellow as ever went between Stern and Stern of a Ship, and can hand, reef, steer, and clap two Ends of a Rope together, as well as e'er a He that ever cross'd salt Water; but I was taken by one George Bradley [the name of him that sat as judge], a notorious Pyrate, a sad Rogue as ever was unhang'd, and he forc'd me, an't please your Honor.

Judge: Answer me, Sirrah, how will you be try'd?

Pris: By G—and my Country.

Judge: The Devil you will. Why then, Gentlemen of the Jury, I think we have nothing to do but to proceed to Judgment.

Attorn. Gen: Right, my Lord; for if the Fellow should be suffer'd to speak, he may clear himself, and that's an Affront to the Court.

Pris: Pray, my Lord, I hope your Lordship will consider–

Judge: Consider! How dare you talk of considering? Sirrah, Sirrah, I never consider'd in all my Life. I'll make it Treason to consider.

Pris: But, I hope, your Lordship will hear some Reason.

Judge: D'y hear how the Scoundrel prates? What have we to do with Reason? I'd have you to know, Raskal, we don't sit here to hear Reason; we go according to Law. Is our Dinner ready?

Attor. Gen: Yes, my Lord.

Judge: Then, heark'ee, you Raskal at the Bar; hear me, Sirrah, hear me. You must suffer, for three Reasons; first, because it is not fit I should sit here as Judge, and no Body be hang'd; secondly, you must be hang'd, because you have a damn'd hanging Look: And thirdly, you must be hang'd because I am hungry; for know, Sirrah, that 'tis a Custom, that whenever the Judge's Dinner is ready before the Tryal is over, the Prisoner is to be hang'd of Course.

There's Law for you, ye Dog. So take him away Gaoler.

This is the trial just as it was related to me; the design of my setting it down, is only to show how these fellow can jest upon things, the fear and dread of which, should make them tremble.

The beginning of August 1722, the pirates made ready the brigantine, and came out to sea, and beating up to windward, lay in the track for their correspondent in her voyage to Jamaica, and spoke with her; but finding nothing was done in England in their favor, as 'twas expected, they returned to their consorts at the island with the ill news, and found themselves under a necessity, as they fancied, to continue that abominable course of life they had lately practiced; in order thereto, they sailed with the ship and brigantine to the southward, and the next night, by intolerable neglect, they run the *Morning Star* upon the Grand Caymans, and wrecked her; the brigantine seeing the fate of her consort, hauled off in time, and so weathered the island. The next day Anstis put in, and found that all, or the greatest part, of the crew were safe ashore, whereupon she came to an anchor, in order to fetch them off; and having brought Fenn the captain, Philips the carpenter, and a few others aboard, men-of-war came down upon them, viz., the *Hector* and *Adventure*, so that the brigantine had just time to cut their cable, and get to sea, with one of the men-of-war after her, keeping within gun-shot for several hours. Anstis and his crew were now under the greatest consternation imaginable, finding the gale freshen, and the man-of-war gaining ground upon them, so that, in all probability, they must have been prisoners in two hours more; but it pleased God to give them a little longer time, the wind dying away, the pirates got out their oars, and rowed for their lives, and thereby got clear of their enemy.

The *Hector* landed her men upon the island, and took forty of the *Morning Star*'s crew, without any resistance made by them; but on the contrary, alleging, they were forced men, and that they were glad of this opportunity to escape from the pirates; the rest hid themselves in the woods, and could not be found. George Bradley the master, and three more, surrendered afterwards to a Bermuda sloop, and were carried to that island.

The brigantine, after her escape, sailed to a small island near the Bay of Honduras, to clean and refit, and, in her way thither, took a Rhode Island sloop, Captain Durfey, commander, and two or three other vessels, which they destroyed, but brought all the hands aboard their own.

While she was a-cleaning, a scheme was concerted between Captain Durfey, some other prisoners, and two or three of the pirates, for to sieze some of the chiefs, and carry off the brigantine; but the same being discovered before she was fit for sailing, their design was prevented. However, Captain Durfey, and four or five more, got ashore with some arms and ammunition; and when the pirates' canoe came in for water, he seized the boat with the men; upon which Anstis ordered another boat to be manned with thirty hands and sent ashore, which was accordingly done; but Captain Durfey, and the company he had by that time got together, gave them such a warm reception, that they were contented to betake themselves to their vessel again.

About the beginning of December 1722, Anstis left this place and returned to the islands, designing to accumulate all the power and strength he could, since there was no looking back. He took in the cruise a good ship, commanded by Captain Smith, which he mounted with 24 guns, and Penn, a one-handed man, who commanded the *Morning Star*, when she was lost, went aboard to command her. They cruised together, and took a vessel or two, and then went to the Bahama Islands, and there met with what they wanted, viz., a sloop loaded with provisions, from Dublin, called the *Antelope*.

It was time now to think of some place to fit up and clean their frigate lately taken, and put her in a condition to do business; accordingly they pitched upon the island of Tobago, where they arrived the beginning of April, 1723, with the *Antelope* sloop and her cargo.

They fell to work immediately, got the guns, stores, and everything else out upon the island, and put the ship upon the heel, and just then, as ill luck would have it, came in the *Winchelsea* man-of-war, by way of visit, which put the marooners into such a surprize, that they set fire to the ship and sloop, and fled ashore to the woods. Anstis, in the brigantine, escaped, by having a light pair of heels, but it put his company into such a disorder, that their government could never be set to rights again; for some of the newcomers, and those who had been tired with the trade, put an end to the reign, by shooting Tho. Anstis in his hammock, and afterwards the quartermaster, and two or three others; the

rest submitting, they put in irons, and surrendered them up, and the vessel, at Curacao, a Dutch settlement, where they were tried and hanged; and those concerned in delivering up the vessel, acquitted.

But to return to Captain Fenn, he was taken straggling with his gunner and three more, a day or two after their misfortune, by the man-of-war's men, and carried to Antigua, where they were all executed, and Fenn hanged in chains. Those who remained, stayed some time in the island, keeping up and down in the woods, with a hand to look out; at length providence so ordered it, that a small sloop came into the harbor, which they had got aboard of, except two or three Negroes, and those they left behind. They did not think fit to pursue any further adventures, and therefore unanimously resolved to steer for England, which they accordingly did, and in October last came into Bristol Channel, sunk the sloop, and getting ashore in the boat, dispersed themselves to their abodes.

chapter 10

Captain John Halsey

J ohn Halsey was a Boston man, of New England, commanded the *Charles*, brigantine, and went out with a commission from the governor, to cruise on the banks of Newfoundland, where he took a French banker, which he appointed to meet him at Fayal; but missing his prize here, he went among the Canary Islands, where he took a Spanish barcalonga, which he plundered and sunk; from thence he went to the island of Bravo, one of the Cape-de-Verds, where he wooded and watered, turned ashore his lieutenant, and several of his men here running away from him, the governor sent them on board again, his commission being as yet in force. From hence he stood away to the southward, and doubling the Cape of Good Hope, made for Madagascar and the Bay of Augustin, where he took in wood and water, with some straggling seamen, who were cast away in the *Degrave Indiamen*, Capt. Young, commander. After this, he shaped his course for the Red Sea, and met with a Dutchman of 60 guns, coming from Mocha, whom he kept company with a week. Though he was resolved upon turning pirate, he intended to rob only the Moor ships, which occasioned a dispute between him and his men; they insisting on the ship's being a Moor, and he asserting she was Dutch, was positive in his resolve of meddling with no European ships. The men were for boarding, but his obstinacy not being to be conquered, they broke Halsey and his gunner, confined both, and were ready to board the Dutchman, when one of the crew perceiving he was about to run out his lower tier, knocked down the quartermaster (whose business it is to be at the helm, in time of chase or engagement, according to the rules of pirates) clapped the helm hard a-wether, and wore the brigantine. The Dutchman stayed, and fired a shot, which taking a swivel gun, carried it aft, narrowly missed the man at helm, and shattered the taffarel. The men perceiving they had caught a Tartar, made the best of their way to shake her off, and some were running down between decks, whom the surgeon pricked up again with his sword, though he was no way consenting to their designed piracy. The captain and gunner were again reinstated after they had seen their mistake, and then they steered for the Nicobar Islands, where they met with a country ship, called the *Buffalo*, commanded by Capt. Buckley, an Englishman, coming from Bengal, which they took after a short engagement there being only three Europeans on board, the captain and tow mates; the rest were Moors. This ship fell seasonably in their way, she being bound for Achen, with butter, rice, and cloth, and the pirates, at that time, were in great straits both for provision and clothing. They took the two mates to sea with them, but left the captain and the Moors at Cara Nicobar, at an anchor, and then took a cruise. Capt. Buckley, who was sick, died before their return. In the cruise they met Captain Collins, in a country sloop, bound also to Achen. He had also two English mates with him, but the rest of his company consisted of Moors. Him they carried to the same harbor where they left the Buffalo.

Here a dispute arose among the pirates. Some were for returning to the West Indies, others were against it, for they had got no money, and that was what engaged their search. They parted upon this; one part went on board the Buffalo, made one Rowe captain, and Myers, a

Frenchman, master, whom they had picked up at Madagascar. The sloop's deck they ripped up, and mended with it the bottom of the brigantine that Halsey still commanded. The ship shaped her course for Madagascar, and the brigantine made for the straits of Malacca to lie in the track of the Manila ships. I must observe, that Capt. Buckley's two mates, whom they intended to force with them, were by strength of entreaty, permitted to go away with a canoe. In these straits, they met an European built ship, of 26 guns, which they had not the courage to attack, being soured by the Dutchman. They afterwards stood in shore, and came to an anchor. A few days after they made a vessel, which they supposed a China junk, and gave chase, but when they came pretty nigh, notwithstanding the pilot assured them she was what they supposed, they swore it was a Dutchman, and would not venture upon him; so leaving off their chase they stood in shore, and came again to an anchor under the peninsula. They lay here some days, and then spied a tall vessel, which they chased, and which proved to be the *Albemarle* East Indiaman, Capt. Bews, commander, coming from China. They came up with him, but thinking it too warm a ship after exchanging a few shot, the brigantine made off, and the *Albemarle* chased in her turn. They however got clear, having a better share of heels, and came again to an anchor. Having not above 40 hands, the water growing scarce, and not daring to venture ashore for fear of the Dutch, a council was called, and it was resolved to make the best of their way to Madagascar, to pick up more hands, refresh, and set out on new adventures. Pursuant to this resolution, they steered for that island, but fell in their way on Mascarenhas, where, making a small present to the governor, they were supplied with what they wanted. From hence they went to a place on Madagascar, called by the pirates Hopeful Point; by the natives, Harangby, near the island of St Mary's in the lat. of 17, 40, S., where they met with the *Buffalo*, and the *Dorothy*, a prize, made by Capt. Thomas White and his company, being about 90 or 100 men, settled near the same place, in petty governments of their own, having some of them 5 or 600, some 1,000

Negro subjects, who acknowledged their sovereignty. Here they again repaired their brigantine, took in provisions and all necessaries, augmented their company to about 100 men, and set out for the Red Sea. They touched at Johanna, and there took in a quantity of goats and cocoa nuts for fresh provisions, and thence in eleven days reached the Straits of Babelmandel. They had not cruised here many days, when they spied the Moorish fleet from Mocha and Jufa, consisting of 25 sail, which they fell in with, and had been taken, if their oars had not helped them off, it falling a dead calm. They had not apprehended the danger so great, if they had not judged these ships convoyed by some Portuguese men-of-war. Some days after this, they met a one mast vessel, called a grab, coming from Mocha, which they spied within gun shot in a thick fog: they fired a shot that cut her halliards, and then took possession of her with their boats. She was laden with drugs, but they took only some necessaries and 2,000 dollars; and having learned that four English vessels lay at Mocha, of which one was from Jufa, they let her go.

Three days after they spied the four ships, which they at first took to be the trees of Babelmandel. At night they fell in with, and kept them company till morning, the trumpets sounding on both sides all the time, for the pirate had two on board as well as the English. When it was clear day, the four ships drew into a line, for they had hailed the pirate, who made no ceremony of owning who he was, by an answering according to their manner, from the seas. The brigantine bore up till she had slung her gaff. One of the ships perceiving this, advised Capt. Jago, who led the van, in a ship of 24 guns and 70 men, to give chase, for the pirate was on the run; but a mate, who was acquainted with the way of working among pirates, answered he would find his mistake, and said he had seen many a warm day, but feared this would be the hottest. The brigantine turned up again, and coming astern, clapped the *Rising Eagle* aboard, a ship of 16 guns, and the sternmost. Though they entered their men, the *Rising Eagle* held them a warm dispute for three-quarters of an hour, in which Capt. Chamberlain's chief mate and several others were killed, the purser was wounded, jumped overboard and drowned. In the meanwhile the other ships called to Capt. Jago to board the pirate; who bearing away to clap him aboard, the pirate gave him a shot, which raked him fore and aft, and determined Capt. Jago to get out of danger, for he run away with all the sail he could pack, though he was fitted out to protect the coast against pirates. His example was followed by the rest, every one steering a different coast. Thus they became masters of the *Rising Eagle*. I cannot but take notice, that the second mate of the *Rising Eagle*, after quarters were called for, fired from out the forecastle, and killed two of the pirates, one of whom was the gunner's consort, who would have revenged his death by shooting the mate, but several Irish and Scots, together with one Capt. Thomas White, once a commander among the pirates, but then a private man, interposed and saved him, in regard that he was an Irishman. They examined the prisoners to know which was the ship from Jufa that had money on board, and having learned it was the *Essex*, they gave chase, came up with her, joisted the bloody flag at the main masthead, fired one single gun, and she struck, though she was fitted for close quarters, and there was not on board the brigantine above 20 hands, and the prize was astern so far, that her topmast scarce appeared out of the water. In chasing this ship, they passed the other two, who held the fly of their ensigns in their hands ready to strike. When the ship had struck, the captain of her asked, who commanded the brigantine? He was answered, Capt. Halsey. Asking again, who was quarter master? He as told Nathaniel North, to whom he called, as he knew him very well. North, learning his name was Punt, said, "Capt. Punt, I am sorry you are fallen into our hands." He was civilly treated, and nothing belonging to himself or the English gentlemen, who were passengers, touched, though they made bold to lay hands on £40,000 in money, belonging to the ship. They had about £10,000 in money out of the *Rising Eagle*. They discharged the *Essex*, and with the other prize and the brigantine, steered for Madagascar, where they arrived and shared their booty. Some of the passengers, who had been so well treated, came afterwards with a small ship from India (with license from the governor of Madras) called the Greyhound, laden with necessaries, in hopes to barter with the pirates for the dry goods they had taken, and recover them at an easy rate. They were received very kindly, an invoice of their goods was asked, the goods agreed for, shared and paid in money and bale goods. In the mean while came in a ship from Scotland, called the *Neptune*, 26 guns, 54 men, commanded by Capt. Miller, with a design to slave, and to go thence to Batavia to dispose of her Negroes (having a supercargo on board, brought up among the Dutch) and thence to Malacca, to take on board the cargo of a ship, called the *Speedwell*, lost on her return from China; but finding here another ship trading with the pirates, and having many necessaries, French brandy, Madiera wine, and English stout on board, Capt. Miller thought it better to trade for money than slaves. The merchants of the *Greyhound*, nettled to see any but themselves take money, for the pirates never haggled about a price, told them they could not do the governor of Madras a more grateful piece of service than to make prize of the *Neptune*, which was a ship fit for that purpose. To which some of the Scotch and Irish answered they had not best put such a de-

sign on foot, for if the company once got it into their heads to take one, they would go nigh to take both ships. In short time after came on a hurricane, which obliged the *Neptune* to cut away all her masts, and lost the three ships belonging to the pirates, which was their whole fleet. They having now no ship, and several of them no money, having been stripped at play, their thoughts were bent on the *Neptune*. The chief mate of her, Daniel Burgess, who had a spleen to the captain, joining privately with the pirates (among whom he died) got all the small masts and yards ashore; and the pirates being requested to find him proper trees for masting, told Capt. Miller they had found such as would serve his turn, desiring he would take a number of hands ashore to get them down to the water, which (he suspecting no harm) accordingly did, and he and his men were seized, and the long boat detained ashore. The captain was forced to send for the second mate, and afterwards for the gunner; the mate, who was the captain's brother, went, but the gunner, suspecting foul play, refused. In the evening, Burgess came on board, and advised the surrender of the ship, which, though but sixteen were left on board, they scrupled, and proposed going under the cover of their own guns to fetch their topmast and yards, and with them put to sea; but the chief mate, Burgess, whose villainy was not then known, persuaded them to give up a ship they could neither defend nor sail; which was no small satisfaction to the *Greyhound*, little thinking how soon they would meet with the same treatment; for two days after, the pirates manned the *Neptune*'s pinnace, seized the *Greyhound*, took away all the money they had paid, and shifting out of the *Neptune* ten pipes of Madeira, with two hogsheads of brandy, into the *Greyhound*, and putting on board the captain, second mate, boatswain and gunner of the *Neptune*, and about fourteen of her hands, ordered her to sea. The rest of the *Neptune*'s company being young men fit for their purpose, they detained, most of whom, by hard drinking, fell into distempers and died. As to Capt. Halsey, while the Scotch ship was fitting, he fell ill of a fever, died and was buried with great solemnity and ceremony; the prayers of the church of England was read over him, colors were flying, and his sword and pistol laid on his coffin, which was covered with a ship's jack; as many minute guns fired as he was years old, viz., 46, and three English volleys, and one French volley of small arms. He was brave in his person, courteous to all his prisoners, lived beloved, and died regretted by his own people. His grave was made in a garden of water-melons, and fenced in with palisades to prevent his being rooted up by the wild hogs, of which there are plenty in those parts.

P. S. The *Neptune* seized as above, was the year after Capt. Halsey's death, ready to go to sea; but a hurricane happening, she was lost, and proved the last ship that gang of pirates every got possession of.

chapter 11

Captain John Bowen

The exact time of this person's setting out I am not certain of. I find him cruising on the Malabar coast in the year 1700, commanding a ship called the *Speaker*, whose crew consisted of men of all nations, and their piracies were committed upon ships of all nations likewise. The pirates here met with no manner of inconveniences in carrying on their designs, for it was made so much a trade, that the merchants of one town never scrupled the buying commodities taken from another, though but ten miles distant, in a public sale, furnishing the robbers at the same time with all necessaries, even of vessels, when they had occasion to go on any expedition, which they themselves would often advise them of.

Among the rest, an English East Indiaman, Capt. Coneway, from Bengal, fell into the hands of this crew, which they made prize of, near Callequilon. They carried her in, and put her up to sale, dividing the ship and cargo into three shares; one-third was sold to a merchant, native of Callequilon aforesaid, another third to a merchant of Porca, and the other to one Malpa, a Dutch factor.

Loaded with the spoil of this and several country ships they left the coast, and steered for Madagascar; but in their voyage thither, meeting with adverse winds, and, being negligent in their steerage, they ran upon St. Thomas's reef, at the island of Mauritius, where the ship was lost; but Bowen and the greatest part of the crew got safe ashore.

They met here with all the civility and good treatment imaginable. Bowen was complimented in a particular manner by the governor, and splendidly entertained in his house; the sick men were got, with great care, into the fort, and cured by their doctor, and no supplies of any sort, wanting for the rest. They spent here three months, but yet resolving to set down at Madagascar, they bought a sloop, which they converted into a brigantine, and about the middle of March 1701, departed, having first taken formal leave of the governor, by making a present of 2,500 pieces of eight; leaving him, besides, the wreck of their ship, with the guns, stores, and everything else that was saved. The governor, on his part, supplied them with necessaries for their voyage, which was but short, and gave them a kind invitation to make that island a place of refreshment in the course of their future adventures, promising that nothing should be wanting to them that his government afforded.

Upon their arrival at Madagascar, they put in at a place on the east side, called Maritan, quit their vessel, and settled themselves ashore in a fruitful plain on the side of a river. They built themselves a fort on the river's mouth, towards the sea, and another small one on the other side, towards the country; the first to prevent a surprise from shipping, and the other as a security from the natives, many of whom they employed in the building. They built also a little town for their habitation, which took up the remainder of the year 1701.

When this was done, they soon became dissatisfied with their new situation, having a hankering mind after their old employment, and accordingly resolved to fit up the brigantine they had from the Dutch at Mauritius, which was laid in a cove near their settlement; but an accident, that they improved, provided for them in a better manner, and saved them a great deal of trouble.

It happened that about the beginning of the year 1702, a ship called the *Speedy Return*, belonging to the Scotch-African and East-India company, Capt. Drummond, commander, came into the port of Maritan in Madagascar, with a brigantine that belonged to her; they had before taken in Negroes at St. Mary's, a little island adjoining to the mainland of Madagascar, and carried them to Don Mascarenhas, from whence they sailed to this port on the same trade.

On the ship's arrival, Capt. Drummond, with Andrew Wilky, his surgeon, and several others of the crew, went on shore; in the meantime John Bowen, with four others of his consorts, went off in a little boat, on pretense of buying some of their merchandise brought from Europe, and finding a fair opportunity, the chief mate, boatswain, and a hand or two more only upon deck, and the rest at work in a hold they threw off their mask, each drew out a pistol and hanger, and told them they were all dead men if they did not retire that moment to the cabin. The surprise was sudden, and they thought it necessary to obey; one of the pirates placed himself sentry at the door, with his arms in his hands, and the rest immediately laid the hatchers, and then made a signal to their fellows on shore as agreed on; upon which, about forty or fifty came on board, and took quiet possession of the ship, and afterwards the brigantine, without bloodshed, or striking a stroke. Bowen was made, or rather made himself, of course, captain; he detained the old crew, or the greatest part thereof, burnt the Dutch brigantine as being of no use to them, cleaned and fitted the ship, took water, provisions, and what necessaries were wanting, and made ready for new adventures.

Having thus piratically possessed himself of Capt. Drummond's ship and brigantine, and being informed by the crew, that when they left Don Mascarenhas, a ship called the *Rook* galley, Capt. Honeycomb, commander, was lying in that bay, Bowen resolved, with the other pirates, to sail thither, but it taking up seven or eight days in watering their vessels, and settling their private affairs, they arrived not at the island till after the departure of the said galley, who thereby happily escaped the villainous snare of their unprovoked enemies.

The night after the pirates left Maritan, the brigantine ran on a ledge of rocks off the west side of their island of Madagascar, which not being perceived by the ship, Bowen came into Mascarenhas without her, not knowing what was become of his consort. Here he stayed eight or ten days, in which time he supplied the ship with provisions, and judging that the *Rook* galley was gone to some other island, the ship sailed to Mauritius, in search of her; but the pirates seeing four or five ships in the N.W harbor, they thought themselves too weak to attempt any thing there; so they stood immediately for Madagascar again, and arrived safe, first at Port Dauphin and then at Augustin Bay. In a few days the *Content* brigantine, which they supposed either to have been lost, or revolted that honorable service, came in to the same bay, and informed their brethren of the misfortune that happened to them.

The rogues were glad, no doubt, of seeing one another again, and calling a council together, they found the brigantine in no condition for business, being then very leaky; therefore she was condemned, and forthwith hauled ashore and burnt, and the crew united, and all went on board the *Speedy Return.*

At this place the pirates were made acquainted, by the Negroes, of the adventures of another gang that had settled for some time near that harbor, and had one Howard for their captain. It was the misfortune of an India ship called the *Prosperous,* to come into the bay at the time that these rogues were looking out for employment; who under the pretense of trading (almost in the same manner that Bowen and his gang had seized the *Speedy Return*) made themselves master of her, and sailed with her to New Mathelage. Bowen and his gang consulting together on this intelligence, concluded it was more for their interest to join in alliance with this new company, than to act single, they being too weak of themselves to undertake any considerable enterprise, remembering how they were obliged to bear away from the island of Mauritius, when they were in search of the *Rook* galley, which they might have taken, with several others, had they had, at that time, a consort of equal force to their own ship.

They accordingly set sail from the bay, and came into New Mathelage, but found no ship there, though upon enquiry they understood that the pirate they looked for, had been at the place, but was gone; so after some stay they proceeded to Johanna, but the *Prosperous* not being there neither, they sailed to Mayotta, where they found her lying at anchor. This was about Christmas, 1702.

Here these two powers struck up an alliance. Howard liking the proposals, came readily into it, and the treaty was ratified by both companies. They stayed about two months at this island, thinking it, perhaps, as likely a place to meet with prey as cruising out for it, and so indeed it happened; for about the beginning of March, the ship *Pembroke*, belonging to our East-India company, coming in for water, was boarded by their boats, and taken, with the loss of the chief mate and another man that were killed in the skirmish.

The two pirate ships weighed, and went out to sea along with their prize, and that day and the next plundered her of the best part of her cargo, provisions, and stores, and then taking the captain and carpenter away, they let the *Pembroke* go where the remainder of her crew pleased, and came with their ships into New Mathelage. Here the two captains consulted, and laid a plan for a cruise to India for which purpose they detained Capt. Wooley, of the *Pembroke*, lately taken, in order to be their

pilot in those seas; but a very hot dispute arose between the two companies which ship he should go aboard of, insomuch that they had gone together by the ears, if an expedient had not been found to satisfy each party, that one might not have the advantage of the other by the captain's skill and knowledge of the Indian coast, and this was to knock the poor man on the head, and murder him; but at last, by the authority of Bowen, Capt. Woolley escaped the threatened danger, by bringing his company to consent to his remaining on board the *Prosperous*, where he then was.

The *Speedy Return* being foul, and wanting a little repair was judged proper for her to go back to Augustin Bay to clean; in the mean-while the *Prosperous* was to have a pair of boot tops where she lay, and likewise to take in water and provisions, and then to join their consort again at Mayotta, the island appointed for the rendezvous.

The *Prosperous* put into Mayotta as agreed on, and waiting there some time for Bowen's ship, without seeing or hearing any news of her, went to Johanna, but not meeting with her there, they apprehended some accident had befell her, and therefore left the place, and sailed on the expedition themselves. As to the *Speedy Return*, she arrived safe at St. Augustin Bay, at Madagascar, and there cleaned and victualed; but tarrying there somewhat too long, the winds hung contrary, and they could not for their lives beat up to Mayotta, and therefore went up to Johanna, where, hearing that their friends had lately left that island, they steered for the Red Sea, but the wind not proving fair for their design, they bore away for the high land of St. John's near Surat, where they once more fell in company with their brethren of the *Prosperous*.

They cruised together as was first agreed on, and after some time they had sight of four ships, to which they gave chase; but these separating, two standing to the northward, and two to the southward, the pirates separated likewise, Bowen standing after those that steered southerly, and Howard crowding after the others. Bowen came up with the heaviest of the two, which proved to be a Moorish ship of 700 tons, bound from the Gulf of Mocha to Surat. The pirates brought the prize in to Rajapora, on the coast of India, where they plundered her; the merchandise they sold to the natives, but a small sum of current gold they found aboard, amounting to £22,000 English money, they put into their pockets. Two days after, the *Prosperous* came in, but without any prize; however, they soon made their friends acquainted that they had not succeeded worse than themselves, for at Surat river's mouth, where all the four ships were bound, they came up with their chase, and with a broadside, one of them struck, but the other got into the bay. They stood down the coast with the prize till they had plundered her of the best of her cargo, the most valuable of which was 84,000 sequins, a piece of about ten shillings each, and then they left her adrift, without either anchor or cable, off Daman.

While they were lying at Rajapora they passed a survey on their shipping, and judging their own to be less serviceable than their prize, they voted them to the flames, and straightway fitted up the Surat ship. They transported both companies aboard of her, and then set fire to the *Prosperous* and *Speedy Return.* They mustered at this place 164 fighting men; 43 only were English, the greater number French, the rest Danes, Swedes, and Dutch. They took on board 70 Indians to do the drudgery of the ship, and mounted 56 guns, calling her the *Defiance*, and sailed from Rajapora the latter end of October, in the year 1703, to cruise on the coast of Malabar. But not meeting with prey in this first cruise, they came to an anchor about three leagues to the northward of Cochen, expecting some boats to come off with supplies of refreshments, for which purpose they fired several guns, by way of signal, but none appearing, the quartermaster was sent in the pinnace to confer with the people, which he did with some caution, keeping the boat upon their cars at the shore side. In short, they agreed very well, the pirates were promised whatever necessaries they wanted, and the boat returned aboard.

The next day a boat came off from the town with hogs, goats, wine, etc. with a private intimation from Malpa, the Dutch broker, an old friend of the pirates, that a ship of that country called the *Rhimæ,* lay them lay then in Mudbay, not many leagues off, and if they would go out and take her, he would purchase the cargo of them, and likewise promised that they should be further supplied with pitch, tar, and all other necessaries, which was made good to them; for people from the factory flocked aboard every hour, and dealt with them as in open market, for all sorts of merchandise, refreshments, jewels, and plate, returning with coffers of money, etc. to a great value.

The advice of the ship was taken very kindly, but the pirates judging their own ship too large to go close into the bay, consulted their friend upon means for taking the said ship, who readily treated with them for the sale of one of less burthen, that then lay in the harbor; but Malpa speaking to one Punt, of the factory, to carry her out, he not only refused to be concerned in such a piece of villainy, but reproved Malpa for corresponding with the pirates, and told him, if he should be guilty of so base an action, he must never see the face of any of his countrymen more; which made the honest broker change both his countenance and his purpose.

At this placer Capt. Woolley, whom they had taken for their pilot on the Indian coast, being in a very sick and weak condition, was, at his earnest entreaty, discharged from his severe confinement among them, and set ashore, and the next day the pirates sailed, and ranged along the Malabar coast, in quest of more booty. In their way they met a second time with the *Pembroke,* and plundered her of some sugar, and other small things, and let her go again. From the coast they sailed back for the Island of Mauritius, where they lay some time, and lived after their usual extravagant manner.

chapter 12

History of the Adventures, Capture, and Execution of the Spanish Pirates

BY CHARLES ELLMS

In the Autumn of 1832, there was anchored in the "Man of War Grounds," off the Havana, a clipper-built vessel of the fairest proportions; she had great length and breadth of beam, furnishing stability to bear a large surface of sail, and great depth to take hold of the water and prevent drifting; long, low in the waist, with lofty raking masts, which tapered away till they were almost too fine to be distinguished, the beautiful arrowy sharpness of her bow, and the fineness of her gradually receding quarters, showed a model capable of the greatest speed in sailing. Her low sides were painted black, with one small, narrow ribband of white. Her raking masts were clean scraped, her ropes were hauled taught, and in every point she wore the appearance of being under the control of seamanship and strict discipline. Upon going on board, one would be struck with surprise at the deception relative to the tonnage of the schooner, when viewed at a distance. Instead of a small vessel of about ninety tons, we discover that she is upwards of two hundred; that her breadth of beam is enormous; and that those spars that appeared so light and elegant are of unexpected dimensions. In the center of the vessel, between the fore and main masts, there is a long brass thirty-two pounder, fixed upon a carriage revolving in a circle, and so arranged that in bad weather it can be lowered down and housed; while on each side of the deck were mounted guns of smaller caliber.

This vessel was fashioned, at the will of avarice, for the aid of cruelty and injustice; it was an African slaver—the schooner *Panda*. She was commanded by Don Pedro Gilbert, a native of Catalonia, in Spain, and son of a grandee; a man thirty-six years of age, and exceeding handsome, having a round face, pearly teeth, round forehead, and full black eyes, with beautiful raven hair, and a great favorite with the ladies. He united great energy, coolness and decision, with superior knowledge in mercantile transactions, and the Guinea trade, having made several voyages after slaves. The mate and owner of the *Panda* was Don Bernardo de Soto, a native of Corunna, Spain, and son, of Isidore de Soto, manager of the royal revenue in said city; he was now twenty-five years of age, and from the time he was fourteen had cultivated the art of navigation, and at the age of twenty-two had obtained the degree of captain in the India service. After a regular examination the correspondent diploma was awarded him. He was married to Donna Petrona Pereyra, daughter of Don Benito Pereyra, a merchant of Corunna. She was at this time just fifteen, and ripening into that slight fullness of form, and roundness of limb, which in that climate mark the early passing from girl into woman. Her complexion was the dark olive tinge of Spain; her eyes jet black, large and lustrous. She had great sweetness of disposition and ingenuousness.

To the strictest discipline de Soto united the practical knowledge of a thorough seaman. But "the master spirit of the whole," was Francisco Ruiz, the carpenter of the *Panda*. This individual was of the middle size, but muscular, with a short neck. His hair was black and abundant, and projected from his forehead, so that he appeared to look out from under it, like a bonnet. His eyes were dark chestnut, but always restless; his features were well defined; his eyelashes, jet black. He was familiar with all the out-of-the-way places of the Havana, and entered into any of the dark abodes without ceremony. From report his had been a wild and lawless career. The crew were chiefly Spaniards, with a few Portuguese, South Americans, and half-castes. The cook was a young Guinea Negro, with a pleasant countenance, and good humored, with a sleek glossy skin, and tatooed on the face; and although entered in the schooner's books as free, yet was a slave. In all there were about forty men. Her cargo was an assorted one, consisting in part of barrels of rum, and gunpowder, muskets, cloth, and numerous articles, with which to purchase slaves.

The *Panda* sailed from the Havana on the night of the 20th of August; and upon passing the Moro Castle, she was hailed, and asked, "Where bound?" She replied, St. Thomas. The schooner now steered through the Bahama channel, on the usual route towards the coast of Guinea; a man was constantly kept at the masthead, on the lookout; they spoke a corvette, and on the morning of the 20th September, before light, and during the second mate's watch, a brig was discovered heading to the southward. Capt. Gilbert was asleep at the time, but got up shortly after she was seen, and ordered the *Panda* to go about and stand for the brig. A consultation was held between the captain, mate and carpenter, when the latter proposed to board her, and if she had any specie to rob her, confine the men below, and burn her. This proposition was instantly acceded to, and a musket was fired to make her heave to.

This vessel was the American brig *Mexican*, Capt. Butman. She had left the pleasant harbor of Salem, Mass., on the last Wednesday of August, and was quietly pursuing her voyage towards Rio Janeiro. Nothing remarkable had happened on board, says Captain B[utman], until half past two o'clock, in the morning of September 20th, in lat. 38, 0, N., lon. 24, 30, W. The attention of the watch on deck was forcibly arrested by the appearance of a vessel that passed across our stern about half a mile from us. At 4:00 A.M. saw her again passing across our bow, so near that we could perceive that it was a schooner with a fore-topsail and top gallant sail. As it was somewhat dark she was soon out of sight. At daylight saw her about five miles off the weather quarter standing on the wind on the same tack we were on, the wind was light at S.S.W and we were standing about S.E. At 8:00 A.M. she was about two miles right to windward of us; could perceive a large number of men upon her deck, and one man on the foretop gallant yard looking out; was very suspicious of her, but knew not how to avoid her. Soon after saw a brig on our weather bow steering to the N.E. By this time the schooner was about three miles from us and four points forward of the beam. Expecting that she would keep on for the brig ahead of us, we tacked to the westward, keeping a little off from the wind to make good way through the water, to get clear of her if possible. She kept on to the eastward about ten or fifteen minutes after we had tacked, then wore round, set square sail, steering directly for us, came down upon us very fast, and was soon within gun shot of us, fired a gun and hoisted patriot colors and backed main-topsail. She ran along to windward of us, hailed us to know where we were from, where bound, etc. then ordered me to come on board in my boat. Seeing that she was too powerful for us to resist, I accordingly went, and soon as I got alongside of the schooner, five ruffians instantly jumped into my boat, each of them being armed with a large knife, and told me to go on board the brig again; when they got on board they insisted that we had got money, and drew their knives, threatening us with instant death and demanding to know where it was. As soon as they found out where it was they obliged my crew to get it up out of the run upon deck, beating and threatening them at the same time because they did not do it quicker. When they had got it all upon deck, and hailed the schooner, they got out their launch and came and took it on board the schooner, viz., ten boxes containing twenty thousand dollars; then returned to the brig again, drove all the crew into the forecastle, ransacked the cabin, overhauling all the chests, trunks, etc. and rifled my pockets, taking my watch, and three doubloons that I had previously put there for safety; robbed the mate of his watch and two hundred dollars in specie, still insisting that there was more money in the hold. Being answered in the negative, they beat me severely over the back, said they knew that there was more, that they should search for it, and if they found any they would cut all our throats. They continued searching about in every part of the vessel for some time longer, but not finding any more specie, they took two coils of rigging, a side of leather, and some other articles, and went on board the schooner, probably to consult what to do with us; for, in eight or ten minutes they came back, apparently in great haste, shut us all below, fastened up the companion way, fore-scuttle and after hatchway, stove our compasses to pieces in the binnacles, cut away tiller ropes, halliards, braces, and most of our running rigging, cut our sails to pieces badly; took a tub of tarred rope yarn and what combustibles they could find about deck, put them in the caboose house and set them on fire; then left us, taking with them our boat and colors. When they got alongside of the schooner they scuttled our boat, took in their own, and made sail, steering to the eastward.

As soon as they left us, we got up out of the cabin scuttle, which they had neglected to secure, and extinguished the fire, which if it had been left a few minutes, would have caught the mainsail and set our

masts on fire. Soon after we saw a ship to leeward of us steering to the SE the schooner being in pursuit of her did not overtake her whilst she was in sight of us.

It was doubtless their intention to burn us up altogether, but seeing the ship, and being eager for more plunder they did not stop fully to accomplish their design. She was a low strait schooner of about one hundred and fifty tons, painted black with a narrow white streak, a large head with the horn of plenty painted white, large main-topmast but no yards or sail on it. Mast raked very much, mainsail very square at the head, sails made with split cloth and all new; had two long brass twelve pounders and a large gun on a pivot amidships, and about seventy men, who appeared to be chiefly Spaniards and mulattoes.

The object of the voyage being frustrated by the loss of the specie, nothing now remained but for the *Mexican* to make the best of her way back to Salem, which she reached in safety. The government of the United States struck with the audacity of this piracy, despatched a cruiser in pursuit of them. After a fruitless voyage in which every exertion was made, and many places visited on the coast of Africa, where it was supposed the rascals might be lurking, the chase was abandoned as hopeless, no clue being found to their "whereabouts."

The *Panda* after robbing the *Mexican*, pursued her course across the Atlantic, and made Cape Monte; from this she coasted south, and after passing Cape Palmas entered the Gulf of Guinea, and steered for Cape Lopez which she reached in the first part of November. Cape Lopez de Gonzalves, in lat. 0 36 2 S., long. 80 40 4 E., is so called from its first discoverer. It is covered with wood but low and swampy, as is also the neighboring country. The extensive bay formed by this cape is fourteen miles in depth, and has several small creeks and rivers running into it. The largest is the river Nazareth on the left point of which is situated King Gula's town, the only assemblage of huts in the bay. Here the cargo of the *Panda* was unloaded, the greater part was entrusted to the king, and with the rest Capt. Gilbert opened a factory and commenced buying various articles of commerce, as tortoise shell, gum, ivory, palm oil, fine straw carpeting, and slaves. After remaining here a short time the crew became sickly and Capt. Gilbert sailed for Prince's Island to recover the health of his crew. Whilst at Prince's Island news arrived of the robbery of the *Mexican*. And the pirate left with the utmost precipitation for Cape Lopez, and the better to evade pursuit, a pilot was procured; and the vessel carried several miles up the river Nazareth. Soon after the *Panda* left Prince's Island, the British brig of war, *Curlew*, Capt. Trotter arrived, and from the description given of the vessel then said to be lying in the Nazareth, Capt. Trotter knew she must be the one that robbed the *Mexican*, and he instantly sailed in pursuit. On nearing the coast, she was discovered lying up the river; three boats containing forty men and commanded by Capt. Trotter, started up the river with the sea breeze and flood tide, and colors flying to take the desperadoes; the boats kept in near the shore until rounding a point they were seen from the *Panda*. The pirates immediately took to their boats, except Francisco Ruiz who seizing a fire brand from the camboose went into the magazine and set some combustibles on fire with the laudable purpose of blowing up the assailants, and then paddled ashore in a canoe. Capt. Trotter chased them with his boats, but could not come up with them, and then boarded the schooner, which he found on fire. The first thing he did was to put out the fire that was in the magazine, below the cabin floor; here was found a quantity of cotton and brimstone burning and a slow match ignited and communicating with the magazine, which contained sixteen casks of powder.

The *Panda* was now warped out of the river and anchored off the Negro town of Cape Lopez. Negotiations were now entered into for the surrender of the pirates. An officer was accordingly sent on shore to have an interview with the king. He was met on the beach by an ebony chief calling himself duke. "We followed the duke through the extensive and straggling place, frequently buried up to the ankles in sand, from which the vegetation was worn by the constant passing and repassing of the inhabitants. We arrived at a large folding door placed in a high bamboo and palm tree fence, which enclosed the king's establishment, ornamented on our right by two old honeycombed guns, which, although dismounted, were probably, according to the practice of the coast, occasionally fired to attract the attention of passing vessels, and to imply that slaves were to be procured. On the left of the enclosure was a shed, with a large ship's bell suspended beneath, serving as an alarum bell in case of danger, while the remainder was occupied with neatly built huts, inhabited by the numerous wives of the king.

"We sent in to notify him of our arrival; he sent word out that we might remain outside until it suited his convenience. But as such an arrangement did not suit ours, we immediately entered, and found sitting at a table the king. He was a tall, muscular, ugly looking Negro, about fifty years of age. We explained the object of our visit, which was to demand the surrender of the white men, who were now concealed in the town, and for permission to pass up the river in pursuit of those who had gone up that way. He now expressed the most violent indignation at our presumption in demanding the pirates, and the interview was broken off by his refusing to deliver up a single man."

We will now return to the pirates. While at Prince's Island, Capt. Gilbert bought a magnificent dressing case worth nearly a thousand dollars and a patent lever watch, and a quantity of tobacco, and provisions, and two valuable cloth coats, some Guinea cloth and black and green paint. The paint, cloth and coats were intended as presents for the African king at Cape Lopez. These articles were all bought with the money taken from the *Mexican*. After arriving at the Nazareth, $4,000 were taken from the trunk, and buried in the yard of a Negro prince. Four of the pirates then went to Cape Lopez for $11,000, which had been buried there. Boyga, Castillo, Guzman, and the "State's Evidence," Ferez, were the ones who went. Ferez took the bags out, and the others counted the money; great haste was made as the mosquitoes were biting intolerably; $5,000 were buried for the captain in canvas bags about two feet deep, part of the money was carried to Nazareth, and from there carried into the mountains and there buried. A consultation was held by Capt. Gilbert, de Soto, and Ruiz, and the latter said, if the money was not divided, "there would be the devil to pay." The money was now divided in a dark room and a lantern used; Capt. Gilbert sat on the floor with the money at his side. He gave the mate about $3,000, and the other officers $1,000, each; and the crew from $300 to $500, each. The third mate having fled, the captain sent him $1,000, and Ruiz carried it to him. When the money was first taken from the *Mexican*, it was spread out on the companionway and examined to see if there was any gold amongst it; and then put into bags made of dark coarse linen; the boxes were then thrown overboard. After the division of the money the pirates secreted themselves in the woods behind Cape Lopez. Perez and four others procured a boat, and started for Fernando Po; they put their money in the bottom of the boat for ballast, but was thrown overboard, near a rock and afterwards recovered by divers; this was done to prevent detection. The captain, mate, and carpenter had a conversation respecting the attempt of the latter, to blow her up, who could not account for the circumstance, that an explosion had not taken place; they told him he ought to have burst a barrel of powder over the deck and down the stairs to the magazine, loaded a gun, tied a fish line to the lock and pulled it when he came off in the canoe.

The *Panda* being manned by Capt. Trotter and an English crew, commenced firing on the town of Cape Lopez, but after firing several shots, a spark communicated with the magazine and she blew up. Several men were killed, and Capt. Trotter and the others thrown into the water, when he was made prisoner with several of his crew, by the King, and it required considerable negotiations to get them free.

The pirates having gone up the river, an expedition was now equipped to take them if possible. The longboat and pinnace were instantly armed, and victualed for several weeks, a brass gun was mounted on the bows of each, and awnings fixed up to protect the crew from the extreme heat of the sun by day, and the heavy dews at nightfall. As the sea breeze and the flood tide set in, the boats again started and proceeded up the river. It was ascertained the war canoes were beyond where the *Panda* was first taken; for fear of an ambuscade great caution was observed in proceeding. "As we approached a point, a single native was observed standing near a hut erected near the river, who, as we approached, beckoned, and called for us to land. We endeavored to do so, but fortunately the water was too shallow to approach near enough.

"We had hardly steered about for the channel, when the man suddenly rushed into the bushes and disappeared. We got into the channel, and continued some time in deep water, but this suddenly shoaled, and the boats grounded near a mangrove, just as we came in sight of a village. Our crew jumped out, and commenced tracking the boat over the sand, and while thus employed, I observed by means of my glass, a

crowd of natives, and some of the pirates running down the other side of a low point, apparently with the intention of giving us battle, as they were all armed with spears and muskets."

The men had just succeeded in drawing the boats into deep water, when a great number of canoes were observed coming round the point, and at the same instant another large party running down to launch; some more on the beach, when they joined those already afloat, in all made above twenty-eight canoes, and about one hundred and fifty men. Having collected all their forces, with loud whooping and encouraging shouts to one another, they led towards us with great celerity.

We prepared instantly for battle; the awnings were got down to allow room to use the cutlasses and to load the muskets. The brass guns were loaded with grape shot. They now approached uttering terrific yells, and paddling with all speed. On board the canoes the pirates were loading the guns and encouraging the natives. Bernardo de Soto and Francisco Ruiz were conspicuous, in maneuvering the Negro boats for battle, and commenced a straggling fire upon the English boats. In them all was still, each man had a cutlass by his side, and a loaded musket in his hand. On arriving within pistol shot a well-directed fire was poured into them, seconded by a discharge of the three pounders; many of the balls took effect, and two of the canoes were sunk. A brisk fire was kept up on both sides; a great number of the Negroes were killed, and a few of the pirates; the English loss was small. The Negroes now became panic-struck, and some paddled towards the shore, others jumped overboard and swam; the sharks caught several. Captain Gilbert and de Soto were now caught, together with five of the crew; Ruiz and the rest escaped to a village, some ways inland, and with the aid of a telescope it was perceived the Negroes were rapidly gathering to renew the combat, urged on by Ruiz and the other pirates; after dislodging them from this village, negotiations were entered into by the king of Cape Lopez, who surrendered Ruiz and several men to Capt. Trotter. They were carried in the brig *Curlew* to Fernando Po, and after an examination, were put in irons and conveyed to England, and there put on board the British gun-brig *Savage*, and arrived in the harbor of Salem on the 26th August 1834. Her commander, Lieut. Loney, waited upon the authorities of Salem, and after the usual for-malities, surrendered the prisoners into their hands—stating that the British Government waived their right to try and punish the prisoners, in favor of the United States, against whom the principal offence had been committed. The pirates were landed at Crowningshield wharf, and taken from thence in carriages to the town hall; twelve of them, handcuffed in pairs, took their places at the bar. They were all young and middle-aged, the oldest was not over forty.

Physiognomically, they were not uncommonly ill looking, in gen-eral, although there were exceptions, and they were all clean and whole-some in their appearance. They were now removed to Boston and confined in prison, where one of them, named Manuel Delgarno, cut his throat with a piece of glass, thus verifying the old proverb, that those born to be hung, will never be drown'd!

On the 11th of November, Don Pedro Gilbert, Captain, Don Bernardo de Soto, Mate, Francisco Ruiz, Carpenter, Nicola Costa,

Cabin boy, aged 15, Antonio Ferrer, Cook, and Manuel Boyga, Domingo de Guzman, an Indian, Juan Antonio Portana, Manuel Castillo, Angel Garcia, Jose Velasquez, and Juan Montenegro, alias Jose Basilio de Castro, were arraigned before the Circuit Court of the United States, charged with the crime of Piracy. Joseph Perez appeared as State's evidence, and two Portuguese sailors who were shipped on board the *Panda* at Prince's Island, as witnesses. After a jury was empaneled, Mr. Dunlap, the District Attorney, rose and said—"This is a solemn, and also an unusual scene. Here are twelve men, strangers to our country and to our language, indicted for a heinous offence, and now before you for life or death. They are indicted for a daring crime, and a flagrant violation of the laws, not only of this, but of every other civilized people." He then gave an outline of the commission of the robbery of the *Mexican*. Numerous witnesses were examined, amongst whom were the captain, mate, and several seamen of the *Mexican*, who recognized several of the pirates as being the individuals who maltreated them, and took the specie. When Thomas Fuller, one of the crew of the *Mexican* was called upon to identify Ruiz, he went up to him and struck him a violent blow on the shoulder. Ruiz immediately started up, and with violent gesticulations protested against such conduct, and was joined by his companions. The Court reprimanded the witness severely. The trial occupied fourteen days. The counsel for the prisoners were David L. Child, Esq., and George Hillard, Esq., who defended them with great ability. Mr. Child brought to the cause his untiring zeal, his various and profound learning; and exhibited a labor, and desperation that showed that he was fully conscious of the weight of the load—the dead lift—he had undertaken to carry. Mr. Hillard concluded his argument, by making an eloquent and affecting appeal to the jury in behalf of the boy Costa and Antonio Ferrer, the cook, and alluded to the circumstance of Bernardo de Soto having rescued the lives of 70 individuals on board the American ship *Minerva*, whilst on a voyage from Philadelphia to Havana, when captain of the brig *Leon*.

"If, gentlemen," said he, "you deem with me, that the crew of the *Panda*, (supposing her to have robbed the *Mexican*), were merely servants of the captain, you cannot convict them. But if you do not agree with me, then all that remains for me to do is to address a few words to you in the way of mercy. It does not seem to me that the good of society requires the death of all these men, the sacrifice of such a hecatomb of human victims, or that the sword of the law should fall till it is clogged with massacre. Antonio Ferrer is plainly but a servant. He is set down as a free black in the ship's papers, but that is no proof that he is free. Were he a slave, he would in all probability be represented as free, and this for obvious reasons. He is in all probability a slave, and a native African, as the tattooing on his face proves beyond a doubt. At any rate, he is but a servant. Now will you make misfortune pay the penalty of guilt? Do not, I entreat you, lightly condemn this man to death. Do not throw him in to make up the dozen. The regard for human life is one of the most prominent proofs of a civilized state of society. The Sultan of Turkey may place women in sacks and throw them into the Bosphorus, without exciting more than an hour's additional conversation at Constantinople. But in our country it is different. You well remember the excitement produced by the abduction and death of a single individual; the convulsions that ensued, the effect of which will long be felt in our political institutions. You will ever find that the more a nation becomes civilized, the greater becomes the regard for human life. There is in the eye, the form, and heaven-directed countenance of man, something holy, that forbids he should be rudely touched.

"The instinct of life is great. The light of the sun even in chains, is pleasant; and life, though supported but by the damp exhalations of a dungeon, is desirable. Often, too, we cling with added tenacity to life in proportion as we are deprived of all that makes existence to be coveted.

'The weariest and most loathed worldly life.

That age, ache, penury and imprisonment

Can lay on Nature, is a Paradise

To that we fear of Death.'

"Death is a fearful thing. The mere mention of it sometimes blanches the cheek, and sends the fearful blood to the heart. It is a solemn thing to break into the 'bloody house of life.' Do not, because this man is but an African, imagine that his existence is valueless. He is no drift weed on the ocean of life. There are in his bosom the same social sympathies that animate our own. He has nerves to feel pain, and a heart to throb with human affections, even as you have. His life, to establish the law, or to further the ends of justice, is not required. Taken, it is to us of no value; given to him, it is above the price of rubies.

"And Costa, the cabin boy, only fifteen years of age when this crime was committed—shall he die? Shall the sword fall upon his neck? Some of you are advanced in years—you may have children. Suppose the news had reached you, that your son was under trial for his life, in a foreign country—(and every cabin boy who leaves this port may be placed in the situation of this prisoner)—suppose you were told that he had been executed, because his captain and officers had violated the laws of a distant land; what would be your feelings? I cannot tell, but I believe the feelings of all of you would be the same, and that you would exclaim, with the Hebrew, 'My son! my son! would to God I had died for thee.' This boy has a father; let the form of that father rise up before you, and plead in your hearts for his offspring. Perhaps he has a mother, and a home. Think of the lengthened shadow that must have been cast over that home by his absence. Think of his mother, during those hours of wretchedness, when she has felt hope darkening into disappointment, next into anxiety, and from anxiety into despair. How often may she have stretched forth her hands in supplication, and asked, even the winds of heaven, to bring her tidings of him who was away? Let the supplications of that mother touch your hearts, and shield their object from the law."

After a luminous charge by Judge Story, the jury retired to agree upon their verdict, and at nine o'clock the next morning came in with it.

Clerk. Gentlemen of the Jury, have you agreed upon your verdict?

Jury. We have.

Clerk. Who shall speak for you?

Jury. Our foreman.

The prisoners were then directed severally to rise as soon as called, and receive the verdict of the jury. The Captain, Pedro Gilbert, was the first named. He arose, raised his hand, and regarded the jury with a firm countenance and steady eye.

Clerk. Jurors look upon the prisoner; prisoner look upon the jurors. How say you, Gentlemen, is the prisoner at the bar, Pedro Gilbert, guilty or not guilty?

Foreman. GUILTY.

The same verdict was pronounced against de Soto (the mate) Ruiz, (the carpenter) Boyga, Castillo, Garcia and Montenegro. But Costa (the cabin boy) Ferrer (the Negro), Guzman, Portana, and Velasquez, were declared NOT GUILTY.

After having declared the verdict of the Jury, the Foreman read to the Court the following recommendation to mercy:

"The sympathies of the Jury have been strongly moved in behalf of Bernardo de Soto, on account of his generous, noble and self-sacrificing conduct in saving the lives of more than 70 human beings, constituting the passengers and crew of the ship *Minerva*; and they desire that his case should be presented to the merciful consideration of the Government."

Judge Story replied that the wish of the jury would certainly be complied with both by the Court and the prosecuting officer.

"The appearance and demeanor of Capt. Gilbert are the same as when we first saw him; his eye is undimmed, and decision and command yet sit upon his features. We did not discern the slightest alteration of color or countenance when the verdict of the jury was communicated to him; he merely slightly bowed and resumed his seat. With de Soto the case was different. He is much altered; has become thinner, and his countenance this morning was expressive of the deepest despondency.

When informed of the contents of the paper read by the foreman of the jury, he appeared much affected, and while being removed from the Court, covered his face with his handkerchief."

Immediately after the delivery of the verdict, the acquitted prisoners, on motion of Mr. Hillard, were directed to be discharged, upon which several of the others loudly and angrily expressed their dissatisfaction at the result of the trial. Castillo (a half-caste, with an extremely mild and pleasing countenance) pointed towards heaven, and called upon the Almighty to bear witness that he was innocent; Ruiz uttered some words with great vehemence; and Garcia said "all were in the same ship; and it was strange that some should be permitted to escape while others were punished." Most of them on leaving the Court uttered some invective against "the picaro who had sworn their lives away."

On Costa, the cabin boy (aged 15), being declared "Not Guilty" some degree of approbation was manifested by the audience, but instantly checked by the judge, who directed the officers to take into custody every one expressing either assent or dissent. We certainly think the sympathy expressed in favor of Costa very ill placed, for although we have not deemed ourselves at liberty to mention the fact earlier, his conduct during the whole trial was characterized by the most reckless effrontery and indecorum. Even when standing up to receive the verdict of the jury, his face bore an impudent smile, and he evinced the most total disregard of the mercy that had been extended towards him.

About this time vague rumors reached Corunna, that a captain belonging to that place, engaged in the slave trade, had turned pirate, been captured, and sent to America with his crew for punishment. Report at first fixed it upon a noted slave dealer, named Begaro. But the astounding intelligence soon reached Senora de Soto that her husband was the person captured for this startling crime. The shock to her feelings was terrible, but her love and fortitude surmounted them all; and she determined to brave the terrors of the ocean, to intercede for her husband if condemned, and at all events behold him once more. A small schooner was freighted by her own and husband's father, and in it she embarked for New York. After a boisterous passage, the vessel reached that port, when she learned her husband had already been tried and condemned to die. The humane people of New York advised her to hasten on to Washington, and plead with the President for a pardon. On arriving at the capital, she solicited an interview with General Jackson, which was readily granted. From the circumstance of her husband's having saved the lives of seventy Americans, a merciful ear was turned to her solicitations, and a pardon for de Soto was given her, with which she hastened to Boston, and communicated to him the joyful intelligence.

"Andrew Jackson, President of the United States of America, to all to whom these presents shall come, Greeting: Whereas, at the October Term, 1834, of the Circuit Court of the United States, Bernardo de Soto was convicted of Piracy, and sentenced to be hung on the 11th day of March last from which sentence a respite was granted him for three months, bearing date the third day of March, 1835, also a subsequent one, dated on the fifth day of June, 1835, for sixty days. And whereas the said Bernardo de Soto has been represented as a fit subject for executive clemency—

"Now therefore, I, Andrew Jackson, President of the United States of America, in consideration of the premises, divers good and sufficient causes me thereto moving, have pardoned, and hereby do pardon the said Bernardo de Soto, from and after the 11th August next, and direct that he be then discharged from confinement. In testimony whereof I have hereunto subscribed my name, and caused the seal of the United States to be affixed to these presents. Done at the City of Washington the sixth day of July, A.D. 1835, and of the independence of the United States and sixtieth. Andrew Jackson."

On the fatal morning of June 11, 1835, Don Pedro, Juan Montenegro, Manuel Castillo, Angel Garcia and Manuel Boyga, were, agreeably to sentence, summoned to prepare for immediate execution. On the night previous, a mutual agreement had been entered into to commit suicide. Angel Garcia made the first attempt by trying to open the veins of each arm with a piece of glass but was prevented. In the morning, however, while preparations were making for the execution, Boyga succeeded in inflicting a deep gash on the left side of his neck, with a piece of tin. The officer's eyes had been withdrawn from him scarcely a minute, before he was discovered lying on his pallet, with a convulsive motion of his knees, from loss of blood. Medical aid was at hand, the gash sewed up, but he did not revive. Two Catholic clergymen attended them on the scaffold, one a Spanish priest. They were executed in the rear of the jail. When the procession arrived at the foot of the ladder leading up to the platform of the gallows the Rev. Mr. Varella looking directly at Capt. Gilbert, said, "Spaniards, ascend to heaven." Don Pedro mounted with a quick step, and was followed by his comrades at a more moderate pace, but without the least hesitation. Boyga, unconscious of his situation and destiny, was carried up in a chair, and seated beneath the rope prepared for him. Gilbert, Montenegro, Garcia and Castillo all smiled subduedly as they took their stations on the platform. Soon after Capt. Gilbert ascended the scaffold, he passed over to where the apparently lifeless Boyga was seated in the chair, and kissed him. Addressing his followers, he said, "Boys, we are going to die; but let us be firm, for we are innocent." To Mr. Peyton, the interpreter, he said, "I die innocent, but I'll die like a noble Spaniard. Good-bye, brother." The Marshal having read the warrant for their execution, and stated that de Soto was respited sixty and Ruiz thirty days, the ropes were adjusted round the necks of the prisoners, and a slight hectic flush spread over the countenance of each; but not an eye quailed, nor a limb trembled, not a muscle quivered. The fatal cord was now cut, and the platform fell, by which the prisoners were launched into eternity. After the execution was over, Ruiz, who was confined in his cell, attracted considerable attention, by his maniac shouts and singing. At one time holding up a piece of blanket, stained with Boyga's blood, he gave utterance to his ravings in a sort of recitative, the burden of which was—"This is the red flag my companions died under!"

After the expiration of Ruiz' second respite, the Marshal got two surgeons of the United States Navy, who understood the Spanish language, to attend him in his cell; they, after a patient examination pronounced his madness a counterfeit, and his insanity a hoax. Accordingly, on the morning of Sept. 11th, the Marshal, in company with a Catholic priest and interpreter entered his cell, and made him sensible that longer evasion of the sentence of the law was impossible, and that he must surely die. They informed him that he had but half an hour to live, and retired; when he requested that he might not be disturbed during the brief space that remained to him, and turning his back to the open entrance to his cell, he unrolled some fragments of printed prayers, and commenced reading them to himself. During this interval he neither spoke, nor heeded those who were watching him, but undoubtedly suffered extreme mental agony. At one minute he would drop his chin on his bosom, and stand motionless; at another would press his brow to the wall of his cell, or wave his body from side to side, as if wrung with unutterable anguish. Suddenly, he would throw himself upon his knees on the mattress, and prostrate himself as if in prayer; then throwing his prayers from him, he would clutch his rug in his fingers, and like a child try to double it up, or pick it to pieces. After snatching up his rug and throwing it away again and again, he would suddenly resume his prayers and erect posture, and stand mute, gazing through the aperture that admitted the light of day for upwards of a minute. This scene of imbecility and indecision, of horrible prostration of mind, ceasing in some degree when the Catholic clergyman reentered his cell.

At ten o'clock, the prisoner was removed from the prison, and during his progress to the scaffold, though the hue of death was on his face, and he trembled in every joint with fear, he chanted with a powerful voice an appropriate service from the Catholic ritual. Several times he turned round to survey the heavens that at that moment were clear and bright above him and when he ascended the scaffold after concluding his prayer, he took one long and steadfast look at the sun, and waited in silence his fate. His powers, mental and physical, had been suddenly crushed with the appalling reality that surrounded him; his whole soul was absorbed with one master feeling, the dread of a speedy and violent death. He quailed in the presence of the dreadful paraphernalia of his punishment, as much as if he had been a stranger to deeds of blood, and never dealt death to his fellow man as he ploughed the deep, under the black flag of piracy, with the motto of "Rob, Kill, and Burn." After adjusting the rope, a signal was given. The body dropped heavily, and the harsh abrupt shock must have instantly deprived him of sensation, as there was no voluntary action of the hands afterwards. Thus terminated his career of crime in a foreign land without one friend to recognize or cheer him, or a single being to regret his death.